The Journey of August King

BOOKS BY JOHN EHLE

FICTION

The Widow's Trial
Last One Home
The Winter People
The Changing of the Guard
The Journey of August King
Time of Drums
The Road
The Land Breakers
Lion on the Hearth
Kingstree Island
Move Over, Mountain

NONFICTION

Dr. Frank, Living with Frank Porter Graham
Trail of Tears: The Rise and Fall of the
    Cherokee Nation
The Cheeses and Wines of England and France,
    with Notes on Irish Whiskey
The Free Men
Shepherd of the Street
The Survivor

The Journey of August King

John Ehle

NEW YORK

In memory of
Vittorio Giannini

A hardcover edition of this book was published by Harper & Row in 1971.
The first Hyperion edition was published in April 1995.

Library of Congress Cataloging-in-Publication Data
Ehle, John
    The journey of August King / by John Ehle.—1st ed.
      p. cm.
    ISBN 0-7868-8031-7
      1. North Carolina—History—1775–1865—Fiction.   2. Mountain life—
North Carolina—History—Fiction.   3. King family—Fiction.
    I. Title.
    PS3555.H5J68   1995
    813'.54—dc20   94-37542
                                                                                      CIP

FIRST PAPERBACK EDITION

10 9 8 7 6 5 4 3 2 1

INTRODUCTION

We begin our lives listening to sounds that are unintelligible and our nights are furnished with coos and croons that help us to find sleep. It is likely that we hear those sounds and they lull us or alarm us before we are even born.

In infancy our brains are formed by the sounds we hear. We begin to create our world and to comprehend our world through the art of language. This is to say that even before birth we are dependent upon the storyteller. As we grow into childhood, we learn to control our fears and extend our pleasures through the stories we hear, through the stories we create, and the stories we believe.

We understand love through stories—from Tristan and Isolde to Romeo and Juliet, to Frankie and Johnny. We comprehend and choose or reject hate and violence because of the stories we hear, from Cain and Abel to Macbeth, to criminals on our evening news. It follows, then, that the storyteller is the link to our world, to the world we have never known, to the world that is and to the world that we would like to see.

John Ehle is a master storyteller. In *The Journey of August King*, Ehle, by telling his story fairly, allows the reader to be the fey young farmer, a terrified young slave girl, and an incestuous slaveholder. John Ehle provides for the reader an understanding of why the principals in his story behave as they do.

The Journey of August King is called a novel of fiction, but I don't believe that is an apt description. I am certain that these events took place just as Ehle has written, for I agree with his statement, "All mountain stories are true."

—Maya Angelou

1 A CREEK IS AN ARTERY of a mountain, though its blood is not salty. The blood oozes through the ground; the water cleanses the body, permits the earth to breathe deep inside itself. You see, most all the water is inside the mountain, not bubbling and cascading and twirling here in sight in the creeks, it is coursing through the ground. It seeps through it and breathes into it, and in this way the mountain lives. A man can make this very mountain bleed by cutting into it with a spade, here, there, in many places. August King can make it bleed in that place where it is soppy now, even though that is not part of the creekbed. Or over there, near those huge tree roots, where the dirt is damp. Most any place down here far below the peaks. And the trees, which are the clothes, the feathers of this massive bird he walks on, their roots sop the water of the mountain into their own veins, don't you see. So do the vines, some of which are grapevines—fox and possum grapes, some of which are ivy. The mountain is a living creature of dirt and rock and water and trees and bushes and vines. Yes, and animals, too, which take the water into their bodies and so become a part of the life of the mountain, though not in the same way as the trees, for they can move to another place entirely if they choose to, either here on this mountain or over there on another one; however, the animals must become part of a place. They must share the life of a place. All beasts, even all men, must. It is wonderfully simple, yet complex.

He used to talk to Sarah about the marvels all around, and his comments merely amused her. He was not a profound man in his thoughts; there was a vagueness about August's mind which he enjoyed, for the world to him appeared as in a glass darkly, or as if reflected in water. No, it was simply that life did not appear to his vision, nor did love, whatever love is; he did not know love, he was vague about that, too. He groped in his feeling, as he did in his thinking. But Sarah was always specific. If August were to say to her that a mountain lives, she would ask how one kills it. You see how simple a question that is. If one cannot kill it, then in what way does it live? "What cannot be killed cannot be alive," she might say, and the utter starkness of the comment would startle him, since it was so simple that it complicated his thoughts. Why did she always seek to do away with wonders and mysteries?

He was on the road on this Thursday when his life began to change, when his life began to crawl from the cocoon in which it had warmed itself for years with its own heart beating. This was after Sarah died, so he had been alone on this journey and was walking home, climbing the steep road back into the deep-forested mountain country, walking at his own gait, which was slow and steady and continuous.

This was October, the month when traffic was heaviest on the road, but nobody was in sight just now, neither bringing their stock down nor their empty wagons up the mountain's wall. And there were no houses or clearings.

Too steep a grade for me, he thought, even though he was lean of body and fit, wiry of muscles and strong, short of stature, well-made; he was handsome, too, with even, sharp features and blue eyes and blond hair which was wispy and unruly over his forehead. He wore homemade wool clothes and leather shoes. By nature he was patient and considerate. He had waited his turn most all his life. Steadily, slowly he had gone about trying to make his way in this world, rarely complaining about his lot or his luck, the ill fate which had denied him many advantages, or even many chances. He was dependable, reliable, steady, which makes his conduct on these next two days all the more astonishing.

His horse pulled the cart with considerable difficulty, for this was a steep climb and the road was rough and rutted. Weary, weary was his procession. His cart's canvas cover was torn in two places, so that it flapped and flipped in the wind, and one of the two big wheels squeaked raspily. His fine, young red boar, following on a rope, snorted his complaints. His new milch cow pulled at her rope, which also was attached to the back of the cart. His dear mare Ophelia's head was bobbing lower and lower, even though the cart was empty except for a few pots and pans, and for three geese, which rode in royal splendor, frequently honking criticism of the wearying circumstance.

Sweaty, sweaty. Tediously, slowly. Nobody climbs a mountainside without loss of strength that he will need in his last days. Mountains are not rejuvenating. They are hungry and seek to take one unto themselves.

"I'll get all of you home," he told the horse and cow. "You might melt into a puddle before it's over, but I will take the puddle home at least."

They had no sense of humor. They were as mournful as Sarah had been in earlier years, walking up this same steep road.

A small herd of cattle and two or three goats, they and two young men and a little, straggly-haired girl, perhaps their sister, waited at the gap for him to arrive and clear the road, then with a wasp of noisy commands they moved on past and down. August stopped his cart in the shade of a big hickory tree, sat down wearily, willing to waste a breath of time for his own comfort. He rested against the hoary trunk and thanked the good Lord he would not have that climb to make again until next year. He wiped perspiration from his eyes and off his face and neck, using his coat sleeve, for he had no extra cloth with him. "Good cold water," he said to his mare. "I need cold water to douse my head in, how about you?"

His young Jersey cow was in anguish from the climb. She had not eaten much today anyway, and her lungs were not accustomed to any such strain as this—though they were not in a high atmosphere as yet, they were at three thousand feet, with mountains rising above them another two or three thousand feet. The cow stood like a statue of a drugged animal wondering just where in the world she was and just where in the world she was going.

He sat with a tree to his back, his legs stretched out before him, looking out over the lowlands, dotted here and there with houses and fields, but mostly cloaked in oaks and other hardwoods. There were many houses, far more than in this wild mountain country, but few villages. August had been born off there to the east a hundred miles away. He had lived there until he was about thirty-five, when he admitted he was not able in that place to break through the set way things were. All the land was owned by tightfisted men and women, who out of love of land or love of their descendants would not part with any of it. His own father had only enough land to keep his family fed; naturally he would not give it to August, nor to any other child, though they were all welcome to live there, it was their home, even August's home at thirty-five, when one evening he said to his two brothers, "Look here, I think I'll go west and try to make a start, even on wild land."

He and Sarah had married down there, off to the east. He wanted a woman who could work, and she could work. Lord, yes, Sarah worked. And she married him conscious of the unemotional way he felt, and she feeling much the same. That is, she would cook for him, tend to him, make cloth and do certain chores. Both of them would work to make a living for their expected family and for each other. So they were married and came up the road, this road, past this very tree, though August remembered few details of the first journey. He did recall his astonishment that anybody would ever climb way up here. He and Sarah went along this road toward the west, to where it joins a north-south road near an Inn, which back then was merely two cabins and two barns. Sight unseen he and Sarah bought from the Innkeeper a parcel of land which was located a few days' journey to the north.

He looked off there at the lowland chimneys, breathing, smoking. Way off beyond sight he grew up. Another lifetime, it seemed to him. Way long ago, seemed to him now. Was he the same person, would he say? Am I not consistent with myself? he asked. Am I not much the same now as on that day at the ridgecrest eight years ago? I have persevered, he told himself, unchanged. Was life intended to be so constant; am I in eight more years, almost to the day, to find myself here, at this tree again?

Suddenly there stirred in him an irritability, even a resentment toward life, which would capture a man so firmly and hold him this way.

He moved west on the road, crossing the high plateau, forest-clad, dark and cool, mountain ranges rising on both sides like tree-covered walls. There were only a few farms pocketed in the forests. A tattered, friendly family with a cartload of cheeses went by, moving east. Over to the left, he could hear the creek, which flowed not toward the east, which surprised him whenever he realized it, but toward Tennessee way off.

The October colors were more advanced here than they had been in the outlands. The leaves already had turned yellow and red up here, the maple and poplar and birch. A squirrel came out from the far side of a chestnut tree and sniffed the air. It looked at him for a few seconds, as if trying to decide what he might be—a bear, an ox, a dog, a bush? A combination of a dog and a bush?

"You don't trust me?" he said to it. "Lord, I wouldn't hurt you."

He came to a straight stretch on the road, and when

he had got to the middle of it, which took about five minutes of walking, he stopped and tied his horse, for here he could see that nobody, no thief, was in sight in either direction. He moved into the woods to cool himself at the creek.

The woods were damp and private; the air settled around him like a cool blanket. The huge tree trunks closed out the less sturdy parts of the world. He listened to the forest breathe. I can hear its life stirring, he thought. Sarah had said he could not hear a forest breathe. He had said to her, "You cannot but I can, and that's the difference between us."

When he had been a young child he had preferred red to any other color; he could remember that far back in his own life. When he had been a young man he had preferred blue. Now that he was middle-aged, was in his early forties, he preferred green, just as it seemed to him that God did, for look here at the sight all around. What a gloomy place this woods would be if it had blue trees and bushes and vines, and red trees would give it too much fire and glory for everyday use —though just now the red maple there near the rock is pretty.

He listened to a tree wheeze, an aged oak tree that was here before white men climbed the mountain wall and pushed the Indians away; an animal could live in the hollow of its trunk. Even a man could live in there, though it offered little protection for a human family. A human baby is not as secretive as is a beast's. A human baby squalls openly, makes its presence known vehemently, and a father must build a protectorate that the beasts cannot gnaw or tear through or burrow under. August recalled that when Sarah bore their little girl,

7

even that first night the baby roused the wolves on the mountain up back of their house, and a year later when she lay ill, dying, even then the baby cried too loud for a wilderness.

The creek beckoned him on, and he hurried through the forest, leaping down the hill. He knelt beside it on a slab of rock and leaned forward so that his face entered the mass of water, and he sucked the life-giving fluid into his own body and became for a moment a living part, attached, to the mountain which rose above him. He was one with the dirt and rocks and roots and bushes and beasts.

Lord, it was a cold stream. It was not ninety-eight degrees; it was closer to fifty. It came from deep hollows of the ground. Look how it glistens, he thought, as it sees the sun for the first day. It looks like the sun, yet is not a sun creature, as any touching of flesh to it will tell, for it stings with coldness, the effects of a long time of darkness, where it has been pooled and protected.

He loved the sting of it. He put his head forward into it and let it swirl about his eyes and nose and ears. See how it clings to him even as he shakes the drops of it off of himself and wipes the mist and film of it off of himself and gasps for air.

With a cry he crept forward partway into the water, slopped his shoulders and chest into the water, even though he was clothed, and let the water soak his body and wash over him, cool him to shuddering, to chest coughing, to a stinging skin-burning. He rolled over and cried out from it, from the pleasure of it, and arose and shook himself and shouted out in excitement, to think he could do this to his body, could cleanse it and excite it so that his own blood rushed swiftly, his heart beat faster, faster, as his blood responded to the greater body of blood before him.

He was on his knees, squeezing water from the sleeve of his shirt when he glimpsed a reflection of a beast moving across the creek, or of a person.

He went on squeezing water from his shirt. In a wild place it is better not to give warning, not to give one's own strategy away, certainly not to move quickly. He didn't even glance up until he was set to meet the danger, or to run if needs be.

So on his knees there by the water he saw the girl for the first time, and he saw at once to his immense relief that she was afraid of him, was trying to hide from him, had been trying to hide in a crevice in the rocks. She was a lean girl with big dark eyes that looked like an owl's peering from a dark hollow. Her skin was brown. She had black hair. She had full pouting lips which might be trembling the slightest bit just now.

She watched him suspiciously, ready to flee should he make a move toward her.

"I wouldn't hurt anybody," he said softly, as to a scared doe. "What you doing here?"

She said nothing.

"Can you talk?" he said.

She said nothing.

He felt in his pocket to see if he had any food, just as he would have if she had been a doe or a cub or a baby raccoon. He found only a rind of cornbread. "Can you eat, even if you can't talk?" he said.

Maybe she had got herself in trouble with a man or

9

with her parents and had run away, he thought, or was a black girl who had run off from her owners. It was hard to say.

"Here, bread," he said.

She watched him apprehensively, waiting for a first signal of attack. She was pretty, in a wispy way, but was dirty and was sweaty, he suspected. She did not appeal to him as a woman—she wasn't a woman, but was a scared animal just now. He moved ever so slowly through the creek to the other side and laid the piece of cornbread on the rock ten feet from her feet. Then just as slowly he backed away until he stood in the water again.

She stared hungrily at the bread.

"You can trust me," he said, wondering even as he spoke if he could trust her, for there might be another one or two lurking about, watching him even at this instant, preparing to attack, to steal from him.

She stared at the bread for a moment longer before she came out of the crevice. She was dressed in an undyed, sacklike dress such as slaves are given to wear, which she had tied around her thin waist with a leather strap, and her young breasts filled the dress at the top and her round hips filled it below. Her arms and legs were slender and were exquisitely formed. Her black hair was cropped close to her head, not unbecomingly. She crouched near the bread, then suddenly all in a single gulp, swallowed it.

"My Lord, you'll choke," he said, astonished.

She looked up, surprised to hear him speak so sharply to her.

"I wish I had more, if only to see you eat it," he said.

She wiped her mouth with the back of her hand, her

black eyes watching him, evaluating him.

"How long you been run away?" he asked.

She watched him, that was all.

"You run away from somebody near here?" He knew she must have, for her dress, though worn thin from use, wasn't torn or blotched by traveling. "Where you going?"

She glanced toward the south.

"To the south?" he said, surprised.

A complex pattern of doubt and surprise came to her face, one change of expression confusing another.

"Don't know your directions, do you?" he said. "Yes, that's the wrong direction for such as you. And I tell you, it's a long way northward, if you go to where niggers are free."

She watched him speculatively, doubtful of him.

"I go north myself for another two days, then the road turns into a trail, and that trail gets ever more straggly once it enters Virginia."

She was listening, was attentive to every word, standing in the sunlight scratching at bug-bites on her arm and frowning at him.

"What you would do is go along this creek to the north-south road. That's where the Inn is. And there you would turn north, up that way to the right, and go two days' journey until the road becomes a trail, which is where I live, and after five, ten days more, you might be to the North. I don't know for certain."

She continued to study him intently, her dark eyes brooding, glancing, wondering.

"I don't know how you'd know when you arrived in the North. I don't even know what Virginia looks like," he said. The wind gushed for a moment, swept through

11

the tree limbs above him. "But I tell you this, it's a long, hard trip for a girl."

"You he'p me?" she asked, her voice soft and husky, the question asked tentatively, her manner already assuming the rejection that he must make; it was as if she were merely hoping that he would not be crude or unkind in rejecting her.

"I—don't very often help other people, except at home, in my own place," he said hesitantly. "I'm not adventuresome." It had been such a mild request from so desperate a creature that it endeared her to him. He would certainly like to help her. "It's against the law," he said.

The low sun, the fading light fell on her head and shoulders and outlined her body, a small, slender figure of a scared woman, really a girl, biting her lip and studying him, her dark, dark eyes puzzling over him.

"I hope you understand about me," he said.

She said nothing.

"I wish I had more bread to give you," he said. He was ashamed simply to leave her. His nature was to be helpful to any creature, but he couldn't get involved with a situation like this. Awkwardly he turned and splashed out of the creek and climbed the bank, but he turned toward her again, attracted to her by her aloneness, her need of him. Even at this meeting he was drawn to her because of himself. He wanted emotionally, desperately to help this girl. "I wish you could understand," he said and turned from her, left her there, tearing himself away from her and, beyond that, away from something inside himself.

Which he supposed would heal.

2 MR. WONDER R. COLE, who started the Inn many, many years ago, had sold August and Sarah their land, six hundred acres for forty cents an acre. That was in 1802. To Mr. Cole they made a payment of money each year, this being the eighth and final year. Also, from his store August would always buy what supplies he would use for the year, would load his cart, now that he was above the steep, long climb.

Mr. Cole was in his store, a room about sixteen by eighteen feet in size, with a dirt floor which thousands of boots had trod into a slick, brick-like hardness. In that room most every inch of space was filled with barrels and kegs and sacks; the walls also were heavy with goods which hung from hooks and nails; even the rafters were almost hid from view by straps and ropes and strings which held more goods, and above the rafters were boards set at random, which were loaded down with goods, too. This was not a store in which one could buy cloth or saddles or furniture or anything else handmade; those items came from craftsmen who lived up here, nearby. What one bought in this store was what he needed day by day and didn't want to haul up the mountain wall for himself.

In one corner stood Mr. Cole, a round-shouldered man in his late fifties, round-faced, pink-faced, a conspiring fugitive from sunlight; he never went into the sun without a floppy hat on. "Ah, August C. King," he said, recalling from memory his full legal name. "I see you've made it through yet another year." He was not pleased, mind you; he seemed rather surprised, as if August was yet another wonder of this wild world: a survivor of it. He took hold of August's forearm, grasped it firmly and shook it with forced friendliness. "Has luck been kind to you?"

He did not say "has God been kind to you," for God suggested unmanageable complications for Mr. Cole. In business matters luck did not demand mercy of him, but the involvement of God might.

"My luck's been fair," August told him.

"Your woman died, didn't she?"

"Ten or eleven months ago," August said. "Died of a fall," he added quickly.

"Oh, yes," Mr. Cole said, staring directly into August's eyes, studying him closely, then releasing his arm and settling back on a tall three-legged stool. "There are many stories about it." He scratched his doughy, pallid face with a long finger. "Fell off a rocky cliff, did she?" he said.

"I brought the money to pay you with," August said abruptly, and took the roll of bills from his boot and counted the money onto the top of a barrel.

Mr. Cole, after wiping his fingers on his shirt, began to make his way through them, counting aloud until he reached the last one. "My, my," he moaned as he finished. "All that work." He wiped his nose and mouth with the back of his hand. "You've got a valuable plantation, August," he said.

"How much will you give me for it?" August asked at once, not that he meant to sell it. Even the thought appeared strange to him.

"Though I must tell you that settlers coming through here tend to prefer to go west rather than north," Mr. Cole said. "The sun seems to call them."

"How much is my land worth now?" August asked.

"I say to them, 'No, no, go north to Harristown where Mooney Wright and August C. King and other such dependable men live, or go to Andrews, where Luther Allen Herman lives.' But they are afraid of the wilderness, as they call the northern woods."

"It's not wild like it once was," August said. "We have communities started now."

"I do want to come see them too, but seems like I never travel more'n a hundred yards from my own lot."

"How much is my land worth? It's not valley land, as I thought it was." As you told Sarah and me it was, he thought. "It's hilly, but there's one flat place up a ways from the webbing of the three creeks, and it will bear a two-acre plowed crop very well. If I ever sold it, how much would it bring?"

"I bought that land from a settler who told me it was valley land. You say it's not?"

"There's no valley on it anywhere."

"I fear the man lied to me, August."

"You told me it was valley land or I wouldn't have bought it."

"You know I told the truth, too, as I thought it to be, don't you? I never would lie over a piece of land, for there's more land in this world than anything else."

"It's rough land to farm, I'll say that. But how much is it worth?"

"As long as you know I dealt honestly with you," Mr. Cole said, picking up the money and putting it deep in his pants pocket.

"For a free man it's all rocks and steep shelves. Even if a man had slaves—"

"You'd think a planter would buy steep land, wouldn't you, since he has hands to work it. Why should they care how hard it is to work? But they won't spend their riches on anything but creekbottoms."

"They don't allow planters near where I live anyway," August said, "not on my side of the river. How much is my place worth, should I ever sell it?"

"I thought Mooney had slaves himself."

"His wife's people had them, but he got rid of them. We don't allow a one on our side of the river."

"I've always liked Mooney, the best in the world."

For a while August stood there, silently reflecting on what they had said and on his dislike of Mr. Cole and his distrust of him. He might as well give up learning about land prices from him, he could see that. "Any slaves run off here lately?" he said.

"Think of that, that you asked," Mr. Cole said. "Olaf Singleterry, he lost two slaves near here day before yesterday, a man and a girl, and he's fit to be tied over it. Not many ever run off up here before, has there?"

"How old a girl?"

"He must be the wealthiest man in this country, don't you agree?"

"I thought you were."

Mr. Cole laughed, a snort with much surprise and pride to it. "I expect Olaf has twenty, thirty slaves, yet he has worried about those two as if his lifeblood was being drained out of him. Afraid his others will run off, as well, I expect. Especially the girl worries him. That girl must be a winner for this world. A little while ago he posted a notice out in the yard, set a reward, put a Virginia riding horse on that girl."

"Lord help us. That's a great deal."

"Men been leaving to go get their bear dogs and come back tomorrow to find her. Olaf was drunk when he offered it, I suspect. He drinks from time to time. Most every day."

August was staring at him, was showing the surprise he felt, and in time he came to realize Mr. Cole was staring back at him, studying him.

"Why you ask?" Mr. Cole said.

"I want a bag of salt," August said. "A hundred-weight."

Slowly Mr. Cole got down from the stool and went along the aisle, which was barely wide enough for him to get through, and brought back a bag of salt, which he laid down near the door. "And what else you say?" he said.

"Fifty pounds of sugar," August said.

"It's right smart dear, sugar is," he said. When August said nothing, didn't even ask the price, he moved up a ladder and pulled a fifty-pound bag down from a rafter shelf, then stood over it, contemplating it.

"I'll need a sack of wheat flour," August said.

"My, you are prospering, August. How much?"

August followed him into the back room, to be sure

there was no rancid odor there, or oil, or water on the floor to contaminate the flour. "A hundred pounds," he said.

Mr. Cole lifted a bag with a grunt. He carried it to the front door, then wiped his face with his floury hands. "What else for you, old friend?"

"Enough powder and lead to last the year."

"Is your gun a Gillespie, August?" he said.

"A piece of one. It's up to the house now."

"Is five pound enough powder?"

"Law yes," August said. "I only shoot at whatever bothers my chickens or steers."

"This much lead?" Cole asked.

"Yes."

Cole weighed it carefully. "Very well. What else?"

"I'll need a fifty-pound bag of coffee beans."

"A pound a week? That's luxury, August, for a single man."

"I like coffee better'n breathing," he said. "How much do I owe you?"

Cole figured up the bill, August watching him carefully.

Then August counted his own money and decided he had enough spare money left to buy a gallon of apple brandy.

Cole called one of his helpers to come load the cart. "Park it where you can watch it for him," he said to the man. "Are you staying the night?" he said to August.

"How old is the girl?" August said.

"I don't know that Olaf said."

August still was thinking moodily of the girl, about having left her; the thought of helping her was still like a painful tooth which he could not stop touching with his tongue. "I'll take the note that Sarah and I signed eight years ago," he said. It was not the girl herself, he supposed. She was not the only girl he had seen this journey, nor the prettiest nor cleanest nor most desirable. It was her fright and loneliness, perhaps, which had so deeply affected him.

Cole opened a pie chest and began sorting through deeds and papers, humming to himself. "I almost forgot to give it to you," he said. He offered a piece of paper to August.

"You might mark it paid," August said.

Cole wrote "pade" across it and offered it to him again.

"Sign it, if you don't mind," August said.

Cole stood there staring at August, wondering about him, speculating about what he thought of him. He signed his name, a scrawl that could not really be read easily, but it was his signature, all right. He offered the paper to August.

"Will you date it?" August asked.

Cole dated it.

"I'll take a bed for the night," August said.

"I don't know the value of your place," Cole said simply, looking off unconcernedly at the cluttered far wall of the room. "I tell you, though, what I understand you have built on it, the house and barn and sheds, the clearing and fences, are worth hundreds of dollars. That's what everybody is seeking now, a place where the grubbing's already done, the fingers are already mashed, the rocks are in place, don't you know?"

"How much it worth, all of it?" August said.

"Do you mean to sell? I have so much to sell, I never buy."

"No, I never thought to sell in this world. I wonder how much I have, what I'm worth, is all."

"Oh, it's worth hundreds of dollars, what you've built," he said, and he wandered on away, dust filtering around him. "There's still too much land, that's the heart of it," he said.

August stopped in the yard at the post-tree and read the notices.

1 doz fancy chairs $1.50 at my place of business . . .
1 rifle gun in shootin shap $6.00 or will trade for salt . . .
3 axes $2.50 . . .
1 horse cart and gaer 20.00 . . .
2 pair fire dogs $1.50 . . .
1 dun colored horse $50. Cum to my house anyday except Sunday with money and your own bridle and saddle or piece of rope . . .
24 volumes of Swift $9.00 . . .
2 volumes of Alexander Hamilton's work $1.50 . . .

Several of the notices were faded, two were faded almost beyond usefulness, both from a Mrs. Cornwall, who wrote that her husband had been lost in the country to the north of the Inn "maybe in a ivy slick and four children and wife wate to home . . ."

There was one fresh notice, pinned over parts of others:

Run off Negro man 19 whip scars on back and butt knife scars on arms and shoulders big lips by name of Sims, reward $50. With him black girl 15, 5 feet 2 inches firm muscled full breasted no scars sound teeth, return her to me unsullied and I will give you my Virginia riding horse Samson Lee or $200, your choice.

Olaf Singleterry,
Hobbs Community near Harristown

Two hundred dollars, or a mount perhaps worth even more in a fancy market town down east. Two hundred dollars. The show of wealth was in itself offensive, but so was the notice, the first about runaways August had seen up here. In the outlands they were common, but here the notice seemed to be a scab patched to the clean bark of a new country.

At supper he watched Olaf eat, Olaf the rich, a distant neighbor who could afford to offer $250 reward for two frightened creatures. He was eating at one of two planters' tables. August was at one of four farmers' tables. Olaf was a big eater. On this night he ate several thick slabs of fresh pork loin, several helpings of corn pudding and stewed cabbage, he ate about a dozen biscuits, drank six cups of coffee that August counted. His big butt hung over the bench where he sat eating, his fat face concentrating on his food, both hands busy with forking, cutting, eating, breaking, his mouth with chewing and belching. Now and then he would laugh, a loud laugh, which always surprised August; Olaf's face would light up with pleasure in the wake of that laugh.

He is a big overgrown boy, August decided.

Everybody had the same food; they all ate too much. August preferred the cold turkey to the pork.

He had cold lamb, too—lame lamb, he supposed, for lame stock could be bought cheaply on the road.

After supper he stopped on the porch, was standing there looking out at the feed yard where big corn wagons were rolling back and forth now, two blacks shoveling corn into the pens. Several farmers were sitting on the ground near him, listening to a banjo picker. He was standing there wondering what he would do with a Virginia horse, assuming he decided he wanted to say where the girl could be found. After all, he did know, and he knew, too, that she couldn't very well expect ever to reach the North. He was bothering himself with such thoughts when Olaf stopped beside him. August spoke to him, the last man on earth he would ever have spoken to normally. "I see you've lost a nigger girl," he said.

Olaf turned his red eyes to look at him. "You got any idea where she is, Mr. What's-your-name?"

August turned away sullenly, struck by the slight, Olaf's rudeness.

Olaf belched. "God, what a meal," he said, and rubbed his sides and stomach, then rubbed his face with his flabby hand. He was a self-comforting man, a sweaty, blubbery man. "I got word of the nigra boy being seen this afternoon," he said. "Two men brought me word they had got a glimpse of him near the road to the north. They chased him into the valley, they said. At least we know he's gone the northern direction. You know, a nigra don't usually know his right from his left hand."

"Is that true?" August said.

"Nor his own name spelled out. They're a sight

smarter than a dog, though, don't you think they're not?"

"I've never known a one," August said.

"I used to tell them which way was north." He smiled then. "Told them different ways." He laughed, that happy laugh of his filled the night air as he stepped down the old wooden steps and started off across the yard.

August slept poorly. He annoyed himself with resentment of Olaf and with romantic notions about himself. Ever since boyhood he had imagined himself at one time or another being a hero, helping somebody in distress, proving his prowess in a dangerous way, perhaps by saving a pretty woman. He lay awake into the night conjuring up fanciful notions about himself, August King, forty-four, a brave knight who came upon this pretty princess.

His bed was in the room adjoining the kitchen, the warmest bedroom in any of the buildings. Generally this room was used by planters, but there was no absolute policy separating farmers and planters; the farmers would not have consented to a policy, though they generally did choose their own, separate tables and rooms as a matter of habit and preference. August went to this planters' room because Olaf was there. He knew Olaf was there, for Olaf had put his big bundle of clothes and scents and soap on one of the four beds. For some reason beyond thought, August wanted to be near him. He had a secret which was of value to Olaf, and that gave August power over him; it was a secret which he would not reveal because of a moral reason, and even that gave him a sense of rightness and righteousness. He wanted to be near Olaf Singleterry and not give him the secret and bask in the sense of decency he was feeling.

Olaf came in late from the yard, where music was still being strummed. He sat on his bed, which was opposite August's, and for several minutes moaned to himself, trying to content himself. He took off his shoes and scratched his feet, still moaning. He had had a great deal too much to drink. He belched repeatedly, a slobbery sound from down in the maws of his flesh. He finally fell back fully clothed on the bed and went to sleep.

August had no use for members of two professions: planters and hunters. He had found both to be selfish creatures, in the main, seeking always to satisfy their insatiable cravings. One was neat and soap washed, the other was grimy and fat soaked. One would watch a slave suffocate for lack of attention, suffocate without family or affection, the other would kill a bear merely to get its liver and would chomp on it raw as he walked on. August disliked, distrusted both sets of men and preferred his own, the earthy, dirt-poor farmers from Scotland and England and Germany who struggled with the land, using their own hands, living with their own families. The land redeemed them. It even cleansed them. It's true, its hardness and its demands ultimately killed them, but then the land absorbed them, which was fair, or at least had a sense of rightness to it, August felt.

August's father had hated planters. He had feared hunters, and he had been afraid of blacks. He told August once that he had never touched a black. Nor had August. Living in the South, in North Carolina, all his life, living near them, never having touched their flesh at all, even in passing, even while working near them at the mill unloading corn or loading meal, or at the forge, where one of them named Jim Henly usually helped the smith with his work, never having touched his arm. Jim was a free black actually. Neither August nor his father, even as a boy on a road, a path, a bridge, at a fort, had touched a black person's flesh.

August lay in bed thinking about touching that girl's flesh. How coarse was her flesh? He groped in sleepy darkness to touch her. How wiry was the hair of a slave's head? Her thighs, what was the touch of the moist hair of the slave's thighs? The thought sent a shudder through him. He could save her, then she could be his slave.

Do blacks also dream of owning slaves? he wondered.

He would deny himself any pleasure of her body, he thought, as his religion demanded, as his sense of decency required of him.

He felt excited and pleased and guilty because of his thoughts, lying not six feet from Olaf, who lay sprawled out on the bed like a massive bear whose liver had just been cut out.

They say Olaf bought his land for five cents an acre. That was in 1790, or some such year. It must have been twenty years ago, at least that long, well before August migrated up here. Olaf bought an entire south cove, with steep mountain walls on three sides of it. He owned about three thousand acres, an entire watershed. There are trout in his streams two pounds in weight, which tells you how large and luxurious his streams are. He doesn't plow or plant any of the steep land; he only uses the broad bottomland along the central creek, which is flat as a table. He has no fences, except along the open end of his holdings, for the wild forest and steep mountains deter any steer or horse from leaving by another way. His place is on the south side of the river, where slavery is by common agreement permitted. His place is about five miles downriver from Harristown, is actually nearer Hobbs.

Well, sir, Mound of Blubber sleeping beside me, August thought, I know something you want to know, something that would cause you and your lordly kind to pay attention to me at last, but you'll not find it out from me, formally known as "What's-your-name," for I am a Christian gentleman who would prefer to help your slaves, even though I fear them, as my father did.

His mind grew more and more drowsy.

A riding horse, what would I do with a horse? he thought. A girl, what would I do with a pretty, brown-skinned girl? A horse for a girl. A girl for a horse. A girl for a whore. A whore for a horse. A horse for a whore.

God forgive me, he prayed suddenly, feverishly. My dear wife Sarah, forgive me for my thoughts, as you must also for my callousness to you while you were alive.

Dawn, barely dawn. Gray light like wash water. The cook started fussing about the kitchen fire. August heard the crackling sounds of grease in the next room. Ham frying. Lame pig frying, he supposed. He heard the cook say, "Get them cornbreads in the oven," and realized the cook was a black man himself. A black man touching my food will never touch me. What song is that? August wondered.

He dozed off and was awakened by the sound of bear dogs barking and sat up, remembering that bear dogs had been sent for, thinking My lord they have caught her, and he sprang half naked to the door and threw it open, and said to a herder outside in the yard, "Who caught her? Who caught her?"

The herder looked up at him, surprised.

Nobody had been caught apparently. Limply August came back inside, embarrassed. Silently he accepted the complaints of one of the men in the room and crawled back into the bed, asking himself, August, what the world is the matter with you? You must have a fever. You need Sarah, bless her, to feel your forehead and look at your tongue. You have made a fool of yourself again.

He cocooned himself under the warm covers and allowed himself to rub his body, the warm skin of his own body, allowed himself to comfort himself, thinking of the girl who needed him.

The dogs would find her, would fell her as she fled. Unless he helped her. He could go to her, take her by the hand, brown hand, and lead her away from where the dogs could track her, up a little branch to wash away the scent of her feet, brown feet. He would even touch her arm, perhaps—brown arm, forbidden arm, black arm, but would not touch her waist, not even to hold her waist so she would not fall, his slave-girl-woman, his girl-woman-slave.

"I feel so bad," his mother once had said, "when they set the dogs on them."

Away from the dogs he could lead her, frightened child, her hand nervously, tightly, clutching his hand, her damp hand, brown black hand, her fingers entwining now in his damp fingers.

She slips. I help her to her feet again, her brown black feet, naked. She is standing close to me, as close as her brown skin.

"I will help you," he whispers to her, into his dirty pillow on his next-to-Olaf bed.

As he dressed, the coldness of the room sobered him somewhat. You should be ashamed of your dreams, August, he said. Are you not a Christian? Did Jesus die in vain? Are all the writings of New Testament disciples lost on you? You are shameless, sinful man, particularly of a night.

"Shut the damn door, mister," one of the planters said.

He shut the door as he left. From the porch he could look down the creek toward where she was hiding. In the yard before him two Hobbs hunters, mean and tough of face, lean and young of body, crouched near the post-tree, eating biscuits and coldly staring at each passerby, at each man who went into the dining hall or came out or went to get his cart or wagon from the guarded pen, watching, studying, looking for a sign that would stir their interest. They were readers of signs. They watched for clues only. They were here for the hunt. They wore leather clothes and moccasins, and were in most ways near-relative of the beasts they normally tracked and killed.

Beyond them, near the store, were farmers with several packs of hunting dogs, the dogs on ropes, snarling, straining, barking, whining, snapping. The farmers stood near them, making plans for the hunt, boasting, laughing good-naturedly.

August was not dreaming now, as he realized, not fantasying. He would not, he could not imagine how he could help that girl. He began shivering like a boy. "Please, God," he murmured, "do not play games with me."

Now, August, he said to himself, you go feed that girl, do at least that. You have to hold your head up in your own eyes. Do that, but do nothing more, for your own sake.

He trembled even at that thought.

August, go feed that girl, he told himself firmly.

3 "WHAT YOU GOING TO DO with all that cornbread, August?" Mr. Cole asked him in the dining room.

He had three big loaves of hot bread, each pone ten to twelve inches across. It was more than one man could expect to eat.

"Can you digest that much meal, August?" a farmer from Burnsville asked him, a man named Turner.

"If it's all I have," August said, "for a two-day journey—"

"Your guts won't dissolve it, August," someone said.

Of course, their noticing him aggravated his own doubts about himself, and when he left them and made his way outside he assured himself it would be better, far better, to go home at once and forget all heroism. Go home and court the Wright daughter tomorrow night—he could be home by dusk tomorrow if he left this minute and traveled as fast as he could.

Yet he knew he would not, could not.

He wrapped the bread in his coat and set the bundle in the cart. He fed corn to his horse and hitched her. He fed corn to his boar and tied him to the back of the wagon. He fed grass he pulled from the creekbank to the cow. He fed the geese corn and pleaded with them please to stop their honking. "I am out of nerves this morning," he told them. They were always upset about any prospect of moving from where they were. They were like old women in that respect. Let a place be broken, sordid, dirty, crumbling, even so they would not consent to move from it. "Listen to me," he told them, "you have the best seat at the party. At least, you're riding."

He was ready to leave, except that the young cow set herself on stiffened legs and bawled to be milked.

"Honey, you've not got any milk in you to speak of," he told her. "And I've got to hurry just now, if I feed that girl."

She wouldn't move. Well, he would leave her here, for he must come back this way. But if he left her here, wouldn't she be noticed by somebody, by Olaf, by everybody? Wouldn't there be questions about her, for she was the best cow in the lot? "Can't you wait to be milked?" he asked her.

He milked her, even as the hunting dogs were being divided into packs of two, three, or four dogs each, even as the farmers were dividing the countryside among themselves, arguing, some to go down the creek, some up the creek, some to go along the road to the north, others to the south. The dogs were snarling and snapping at each other and at strangers, flinging saliva from excitement and hunger, wanting to get on whatever trail it was they were to follow, to whatever ripe game.

Across the yard he saw a gray-haired, small Negro, a

warped man come forward with a garment. He approached two white men with it. The men sniffed the garment and, laughing, threw it to their dogs. The men held their noses, still laughing, and one said, "She was musky and ready, if she wore it."

"Must 'a' been in heat," the other said.

"It'll ruin my dog's nose, I'm afeared," one of the farmers said.

Good-natured joking, pleased and pleasant on this cool morning before a hunt, or so August supposed they felt.

Olaf appeared, a mug of steaming coffee in his hand. "I have offered this horse here," he said, indicating his own mount, which was tied to a chestnut tree nearby, a beautiful animal really, a light roan with a dark-brown tail and mane, perfect legs and feet, powerfully formed shoulders, no fat on her, a proud horse, as befits Virginia. "Now I'll be on the road going home once you find her," Olaf said. "And so'll this horse be."

"You smell that there?" one of the farmers asked him, kicking the garment.

"She never wore that," Olaf said resentfully. "She had a better dress than that, didn't she?" he said to the old Negro.

"Well, does she smell like that?" a farmer asked, and snickered behind his hand.

Good-natured fun, but Olaf was irritated by it. "That's not her dress."

"They all smell alike to me, boys," a farmer from Madison said.

The old Negro, expressionless, stood to one side nodding.

Mr. Cole came out on the dining-room porch, to see what the commotion was about.

A planter said gruffly, "Why do you men laugh? If they escape, the damned roads will be nigger-filled, if they're not caught."

"Can we use her a little bit on the way in, Olaf?" one young farmer said, smiling in embarrassment, his teeth showing, his lips tight.

Several men laughed nervously, then everybody grew quiet; it was ragged and uneasy, the feeling that the question aroused, for white men didn't often admit they might be attracted by a black girl, much less would take one to themselves.

Olaf said sternly, "I tell you boys, all joking aside, I want that girl unsullied, you hear me?"

"Why is she so picked-out?" a farmer said simply.

Olaf considered the man, the question, but said nothing.

"What if she asks for it, Olaf?" one of the farmers called.

It was so surprising a comment and so blatant an affront to Olaf that several men laughed suddenly.

Another farmer said, "Let her suck your finger."

Several men laughed again, although the remark embarrassed most of the men, including August. Olaf said nothing. Like a rock he stood in the yard, staring at them sternly, frowning with the wrath of a fat god. The old Negro didn't smile either. August watched all this as he finished milking his cow, spraying the milk on the ground, for he had no time to find one of his pans, he was so anxious to be gone.

As the men dispersed, there was more whispering

and wonder. One farmer, passing August, holding a seething mongrel dog on a leather leash, said, "Olaf's got nerve to talk to us like that."

"I allow," August said, stripping the cow.

Several farmers were leaving the camp, four or five of them going toward the bridge. Where are the two long Hobbs hunters? August wondered. Hunters always chose their own territory and moved to themselves, and they didn't need dogs to track with, either.

"There's going to be baying soon," he told the cow, "and we'll be mixed up in it, because of you." And he told himself, "August, a knight doesn't have a cow."

He had to laugh, thinking about that.

At the bridge he paid his three-cent fee, a cent for the horse, a cent for the cart, and a cent for the cow. He had got his pig and himself in the cart, so they went free.

Once across, he put his pig out on a tailgate rope and started toward the east, back the way he had come, which the bridge attendant noticed. "You just come from there yesterday," he called.

"I left my knife on a stump," August told him.

"Ah, law, too bad."

"I'll be back by directly." Did he believe me? August wondered. Even if he did believe me, he will remember me, won't he?

Three dogs were fighting. He was glad to see it, too. Dogs usually delayed a hunt to a fare-thee-well. The men had rather listen and watch the dogs than hunt anyway, in his opinion.

He kept telling his dear horse to hurry along.

A family came into view, Ed Coleman's people, all of

his six children strung out according to age and endurance, carrying packs. Ed's wife greeted August with high spirit. "Where in the world you going, August? You've got no stock to sell, except a boar and a cow?"

"That's all I have just now," he said.

"I got the best prices ever this trip," Ed said, stationing himself in the road, prepared to tell moment by moment about his trades of yesterday.

"I'll be going on now, Ed," August said, and moved past him.

Ed called out, "What in the world has got into you, August?"

Even his children called to August, their friend, surprised, for rudeness was inexcusable in this country.

But August went on, knowing he would need to go to their place one day next week and explain, say whatever he had thought of by then to say, and sit with them for an hour or two. In the plight of the moment he simply couldn't stop and didn't know what to say or do.

At the very place, at the same tree as yesterday, he tied his horse and hurried down through the woods carrying a round of the warm cornbread with him, out of breath, more from nervousness than from exertion. When he reached the creek where the girl was, where she had been yesterday, he stopped, stunned, cruelly struck, for she was not in sight anywhere. The great black caverns and the gray rocks rose above him, bleak and uninviting. "Hey, hey, you," he said.

Not a sound, except of the creek gurgling and of the dogs baying up the creek a ways.

"Hey," he said as loud as he dared, thwarted, baffled, for he had imagined finding her waiting for him. "I brought you this," he said holding up the loaf of bread.

No answer. No sign or sight of movement in those towering rocks.

She's here, he told himself. "Hey, listen, I will leave it here on the rock," he said, and he put it down at the edge of the creek. "But you'll need to fetch it before those dogs get here."

No answer.

"Well, damn you," he said, cruelly frustrated, "protect yourself then," he told her, and backed away from the place, finally, reluctantly turning from it, pulling his way up the bank holding to rhododendron boughs, fussing at himself for being such a fool as to come all this way, to risk himself in this manner, all to benefit no person, for no result in the world.

He stopped. Those dogs will get the bread, the farmers might know he had bought three loaves of bread this morning, the bridge attendant would testify he had come this way.

He ran back to the creek and got the loaf. "I'll leave it near the road," he said to the rocks, and climbed the bank once more.

Flee, that's all you can do now, August, he told himself. You are not made for conspiracies, that's clear now. You worry about every notion. Your own doubts multiply and make you awkward.

He hurried as fast as he could, dropping the pone of bread just inside the woods, behind a line of matted bushes and saplings.

With trembling fingers he unhitched his horse, even as a farmer name of Bolton approached from the east, leading two empty packhorses, and called to him in a jesting manner, "What you running from, August? What were you doing in there?"

"What you think?" August said, hitching up his pants, resetting his belt on his hips. He moved his horse onto the road, switched her into motion.

"Say, August," Bolton said, walking up beside him. "Don't I smell cornbread?" he said.

"Out here in the woods?" August asked.

"Fresh-baked cornbread."

"Two pones there in the cart." August took one up and broke him off a piece.

He accepted it greedily and chewed it even as he tried to talk. "How did you get it warm out here?" he said.

"Those dogs sound like they're on a scent," August said, hoping to distract him.

Bolton sniffed the air himself, as if he were a finder dog. "Not on it yet."

"They've not found the scent yet?"

Bolton reached for another hunk of bread. "How'd you warm it, August?" he said.

"I had a dog, but she died two years ago," August said, "soon before my baby died. I don't know dogs well."

"They're coming down the creek," Bolton said. "Four of them."

"Three," August said.

"Oh, hell," Bolton said, and laughed at him. "Four. Don't you know dogs?"

There was tension on their barks now, all wheezened noises, insistent and whiplike.

"They looking for you, August?" Bolton asked, smiling at him, showing his tobacco-yellowed teeth. He was about fifty, a widower, as probably he always would be, for he didn't care about himself and was rotting away now.

The dogs' voices changed all in an instant. One of them, apparently as it approached the place where the girl had been, set up a clear, blood-chilling cry, and the other dogs, all in the next instant, set their voices to the same blood-chilling chorus. Fear swept through August —my Lord, there is no person born who can face dogs like that. He was frozen to the road, while Bolton, smiling, relaxed, stood nearby, his head cocked to one side as he listened; he appeared to understand the messages the dogs made and to enjoy hearing them, much as other men might enjoy music.

"Have they found her?" August asked him, his voice trembling.

"Is it a bear, do you think?" Bolton said.

"Have they found her?" August demanded.

"They're coming up this way now," Bolton said.

"Did she leave the creek?"

"Coming up through the woods there. Better get in your cart," Bolton said, and laughed.

The baying was close, the cruel, bleating sounds were all about them. Then suddenly the voices changed. In the bushes down the road fifty feet away the voices changed into growls and snarls. The dogs had caught their game and now began to tear at it. From farther down the bank their masters began shouting at them, "No, don't hurt her, don't hurt her, don't hurt her."

August ran toward the dogs himself, shouting at them. He waded into the rhododendron just as the dogs broke free; snarling, biting at each other, as they came rolling onto the road, cornbread splattering over the road as they fought for it, snapped at it and at each other.

August sank down on the road, relieved, the dust of the road filtering around him, the dust from their fighting.

"What the hell they tearing up, August?" Bolton said. "Is that cornbread too?"

Three farmers burst out of the bushes and began to swear at the dogs. "Where you put her?" they said to Bolton.

"Her who?" Bolton said.

"The nigger girl."

"Why, hell, I don't know," he said.

One farmer ran down the road to August's cart and searched it, then beat the bushes near it. He came running back. "Did she get away?" he asked August.

"Did you see her?" August said.

"No, hell, no," the farmer said. "But the dogs struck somebody's trail down at that creek." He waded in among the dogs, kicking at them. "What the devil is that they're fighting over?"

"I don't know," August said.

"Ain't it cornbread?" Bolton said.

"Where would they get cornbread?" a farmer said, turning on Bolton angrily, as if Bolton had challenged him.

August started off to his cart.

"This is the queerest place for cornbread I ever saw," Bolton said.

"Did you see that girl?" a farmer asked him.

"That fellow even has cornbread in his cart," he said.

"Did he feed my dogs? If he fed my dogs, I'll not stand for it one bit," a farmer said.

"Why, he never," Bolton said. "I was with him."

August walked at the head of his horse, setting a swift pace, anxious to be gone.

"Who the hell is he?" August heard a farmer say to Bolton.

"This here cornbread's warm," August heard a farmer say.

He heard Bolton say cornbread once more and break into laughter.

It was, August promised himself, the last time he would try to help the girl. It was, as he well knew, his last encounter with her. All very well, let it be that way, he thought. Thank God. No slaves for me, no more adventures for me, please God. Dear God, just let me be.

4 HIGH MOUNTAINS are up this way. They are the highest anybody in this country knows about, the highest in the nation itself, except perhaps out west, where few have ever gone and where all distances are greater. Once August thought about going west himself, maybe as far as Ohio. This was when Sarah died. He thought, Well, August, get on out there to a new start. Leave here, these rocks, these trees so big they won't even burn down or stop sprouting, those two hillside graves . . .

The mountains over there to the west are the Blacks. Those two center peaks are the Black Brothers. See how the clouds gather at the peaks and cling to them. Rains fall on those peaks every now and then, most every day as the clouds strike them. All those mountains have black trees growing on them, which accounts for their name. Twisty black trees, hemlocks or spruce of some sort. Or so they say, those who have been way up there.

The road through here is steep and rock-jagged. It is little more than a trail which years of use have tempered and wrinkled like an old man's flesh and that the rains keep washing over, so that perhaps it will all cave in someday. Nobody lives on it. It leads to settlements, but it is not itself settled. On some of August's early journeys, when he and Sarah had taken their first crops to market, their cattle and pigs to sell, he had lost about half of their livestock on this road, some to beasts, the bears mostly, some to wolves, some to mountain lions, some to falls from cliffs, some to the river crossings, of which there were two, some to the weather, which was stormy and windy in October, subject to frequent, sudden expressions of annoyance, much as men who are aging and dying fall victims of their own temperament, especially of a night.

Some people get up here in this high, wild country and begin to sing and shout. August got giddy himself, especially on a morning such as this, one clear as glass and brisk with cool winds. The forests, too, were full of spells and changing shapes. Their vines and ghosts were everywhere. Look at those hickory trees. Three men cannot reach around their trunks. Look at those poplar trees. Lord have mercy, they're so huge they look like God's legs. Way up in the sky out of sight is God's body standing on those long, straight stalks.

Walk, God.

Go on, let me see you walk.

You're always so critical of others, let me see you try to do something for once. Listen to me, you can take a step that will cover a hundred feet with those legs. You can walk across the valleys with those legs.

God, let me see you.

We won't laugh at you, if it's your first try.

Though you were up there this morning laughing at me, while I was fumbling about with that cornbread. God, let me see you walk.

He can do anything, God can.

Here and there a little trail would wander off to the right or left and there would be deep ruts in it at the soppy places. Down there at the end of it is a family, he would think, and he would try to imagine what sort of house they had built, how much land they had cut or burned to make a cornfield and a grazing place. Most all were poor, he had no doubt, as he had been from the start—though now, without any further payments to make on this land, he was established and had fine breeding stock to make his fortune with.

He had bought this young cow and three geese at Old Fort, at the foot of the mountains, for his cow up home was old and obstinate and needed company, and he had no geese at his place and very much wanted a flock of them, for they protect themselves better than chickens in a wild country. Also, he had bought the beautiful young boar to improve his drove. Every year that he had gone to market he had managed to make a few such improvements in his stock, and he would do better still, now that Sarah had died. When she was with him she always had ideas of her own about how they might spend their money, most all of them having to do with cloth and dishes and glass, substances which, as he had repeatedly pointed out to her, did not reproduce themselves.

"We'll arrive home tomorrow evening, if we walk

constantly and don't tarry, you hear me?" he said to the horse, his mare Ophelia, and slapped her rump, and she bobbed her head in acknowledgment of his attention. A rich sensation of warmth and comfort flowed through him when he thought of being home again.

October was the busiest month of the year on the road, for many families only went to market once a year, and autumn was the time their stock was fattest and they had free time. Twice August pulled his cart over to one side to let small herds go by, one of horses and one of cattle, and he acknowledged the greetings of the herders. He passed three camps. People got a lazy start in the mornings on the road, for they had spare time to use as they pleased, and they needed to let their stock graze and root in the woods.

Olaf had just passed by. Harold Creasy's wife told August that. She was in her seventies, but she still made an annual trek to town and back, to sell a flock of sheep. Just now, on her way home, she was sitting on a bank, taking a rest.

She told August that Olaf and his wagons had just passed. "Why does he take an old nigger woman with him to town and back?" she asked.

"Excursion," August said.

The word meant nothing to her. "It's his wife causes it," she said. "They tell me Imogene gets angry at first one and then another, and whenever he's away she beats on that 'un."

"Who said that?" he asked her.

"I've heard it said," she said, disdaining to admit to an authority higher than herself. "He has this one nigger woman with him that I saw myself, and she's nine months gone if she's a day, which means to me she's not along because he needs a cook."

"Has he found the two runaways yet?" August said.

"He says he's not," she said.

"He seems to want the girl back mostly."

"Don't even want her switched. Wants her cotton-handed back to him."

"Well, planters have their own worlds to live in," he said.

She twisted her brown-splotched hands together, cleaning the road dust off them; they shone with age, were tight-skinned over her bones and looked like bird's bodies that had been defeathered. "I got my ideas about it," she said.

Later August came upon a family which said they had been robbed of their stock. The husband was moody, seemed to be ill. The wife, a greasy woman with coarse speech and a sour smell about her, told August that three teen-age boys had come out of the woods and had taken their money. But even as she spoke, her two children sat on a log nearby, looking about with stubborn boredom, drab and unimpressed, unexcited.

"Well, there's danger most everywhere," August said, whacking his horse's rump and going on.

"Ain't you going to go into the woods to help find them?" the woman demanded.

"Yes, yes," he said, but he went on, walking on the far side of his horse, away from them. He didn't stop, and the woman began to shout after him, calling him all manner of filthy names; she stirred up road dust around her as she stomped the ground in wrath and frustration.

What if he had gone into the woods with them, he

wondered. Would she have taken all he had? Maybe she would only have taken the coffee or the sugar.

Filthy-mouthed woman. It is rare up here to find a woman like that, for most communities won't allow them to stay. Of course, if a community gets out of sorts with a person, that person is in pain, for where will he get medicine if he has a sickness and is without, or a plowpoint if he breaks his, or help with the harvests or the butchering, or help with the birth of his child, or somebody to split roof shanks with him or help him find his cattle or mend his wheel or show him how to tan leather, or do any of a hundred different chores that need getting done, for no one man can know all that must be known in a place isolated from public towns. No, one cannot in a wilderness live alone, and no community in a wilderness will permit much deviation from its own measures, either, from its own personality, for by the community most individuals—for instance, along this road—are evaluated, just as also the value of land in a community is judged by the quality of its citizenry.

So this lady, the one back down the road, she must be an outcast, he thought, and therefore desperate.

And consider this: maybe even God would not bless her with rain, and so in that way too she would deprive her neighbors.

God, why don't you strike her down now? he asked, speaking up into the shafts of the poplars. "Hey," he shouted, amused by his own notions, "walk all over her," he said.

And he laughed at his foolishness. A man who lives alone learns to amuse himself, and amuse his stock.

"There are thieves all about," he told his mare, "so take care or you'll end up in some other man's lot."

The mare nodded her head as if she understood, and he patted her neck lovingly.

It was true, there were certain thieves along the road, particularly here along this northern stretch. Many of them were not thieves by habit; they were decent farmers who had suffered losses they could not afford, and who stood to lose their house, their crib, their barn, their stock, to lose even their land and therefore their chance to make a living for their family. They were desperate, so they stole, but even they would not steal from members of their own communities. In a sense they were permitted to steal on the road; those who had suffered losses could take the lame and sick stock that had been left behind by others, or take strays, or take most anything else which was not adequately protected, the degree of their crime to be judged in terms of their desperateness. They might take a cart, or steal the canvas cover from the hoops, or take one's stock. No one ventured onto the road without knowing this and risking himself to it, as well as to the wild beasts, which operated under much the same system, preying first on the lame and sick, then on the strays, then on whatever else was not adequately protected. The road had established these rules over its thirty years of use; this was its way of life as it snaked its way along, growing more and more narrow and tortured up this northern way.

A dozen cattle were driven past. Directly behind them came a flock of turkeys walking behind their gander, their heads bobbing, their clucking sound a friendly accompaniment to their boredom, until they saw August's boar, at which time a loud burst of sound erupted, a startling noise which frightened both August and the boar and would have frightened even a mountain lion or a bear.

Cattle on the road. A planter must have had a hundred head, and he had two blacks to help his two sons. All of them were walking. "Not going to risk my blacks next year, if what I hear is so," he said to August.

What did he mean? August wondered, but he didn't ask, didn't admit to any ignorance.

"Outland diseases," he murmured to August.

"That so?" August said.

"They'll be filling up the road, unless it's stopped now. Nip the bud, I tell you, or it'll flower."

"I expect so," August said.

A drove of swine came along, led by an old boar. "They will have to make sausage out of you, mister," August told him, then felt bad, for he shouldn't be unkind, even to such a mangy rascal. The boar ignored him proudly, splendidly, but when he saw August's boar he stopped and studied him with his red eyes, then pawed the ground a time or two. August's boar was too young to fight.

"You want to sell him?" a drover said to August.

"No, never in this world," August said. "You mean my boar?"

"He's the best I ever saw," the drover said enviously.

"A man named Curtis Hopper near Marion bred him, had two as pretty, and I got one from him for a dear price. I owe part payment yet."

"He's worth any price," the drover said.

"Yes, I know he is."

"He'll give you the best drove anywhere abouts, if I'm to judge," the drover said, his dusty red eyes staring at August—enviously, without much regard for him, for his success, or even for the boar. He was quite a common sort of fellow, without appreciation for anything except his own lusts and cravings, or so August decided.

Goats. A little herd of about a dozen goats. Two females on ropes and the others following, the two females led by two barefooted girls. Not much money in goats.

"Where your parents?" August said to the girls.

"Coming with the cows," one of the girls said.

"You better wait for them," he said.

The girls must have agreed, for they sat down on the bank, sighing heavily, as no doubt they had seen their mother do. Neither of them was the least bit winded. Pretty girls, had skin like porcelain, long blond hair. "Have you seen ary one of the niggers?" one of them asked August.

"No, not yet," he said. "They must have vanished into thin air."

"Can they?" the younger girl said suddenly.

"Oh, a black can do anything," August said.

She glanced about nervously, as if the ghost, the vapor of the slave was ever so near and might choke her. "Would my goat know?" she said.

"Not unless it's a black goat," he said.

What a fool I am to tantalize a child this way, he thought. What gets into me? He took comfort from the other girl's unconcern; obviously a girl did not have to be afraid of a ghost, for only one of them was.

Their parents came into view. "Have you seen either one of them yet?" the father said to August.

"No, no," he said, assuming he meant the runaways and not the girls, who sat a few feet from him.

Chickens in a wagon. How can anybody make a living transporting chickens in a wagon? Let the outlanders grow their own chickens, he thought. He had more respect for his horse than to demean her that way. And more respect for his cart, which was as sturdy a cart as ever was made—it was built by Mr. Colley in Andrews. August had spent three days with him, persuading him to get around to it; he went to his house and slept on the porch, helping him of a day, insisting on the best ash, the best oak, declaring at mealtimes his intention to remain until he was satisfied with the work, even winking at Colley's wife—a harmless sin, for August had never touched a woman except Sarah in his life. Is it against any rule in the Bible to wink at a cartwright's wife? he wondered.

The cart was made 5 feet 7 inches long, August's length.

Three men eating. "Must be noontime," August said. He stopped to eat a biscuit with them.

One of them said to the other, "You can't find any tracks on a road as traveled as this one, I tell you."

"I can tell nigger tracks whenever I see them," the other one said.

"The devil you can. What's the difference between nigger tracks and human tracks?"

"Toes. Nigger has three extra toes."

August had to laugh. As he went on he thought about the marvel of the human mind, how it could entertain itself endlessly.

He began to sing. He forgot the girl. He felt relaxed and secure, like his old self again.

> When I was a little boy,
> Just eighteen inches high,
> How I'd hug and kiss those girls
> To see their mamas cry!

A crossroads, one little shaggy trail leading off to the left toward a score of communities, some with as few as twenty families in them, some with fifty, as many as that. Few ever had more, for more than that couldn't get inside a church building, not inside any that had ever been built up here.

A potter had parked his cart near the turnoff and was displaying his wares. He was willing to barter pots for lame stock, apparently; for he had a pen nearby, one made of saplings and twigs and the like, and inside it he had a mangy turkey, two bony pigs, and a bawling calf. The potter lived near Harristown. His name was Flax. He called to August, to ask him how well he had done in the outlands and to ask about the two runaways. The potter said he wished he could find either one of them. "I could get out of debt if I found the girl," he said, "but I'll take ary one, mind you, and not be greedy."

He had about fifteen pots beside the road and others in his cart. He had a hooped canvas cover over the cart, too, just as August did; his cart had been made by the same man. The pots were mostly jugs, but he had a four-gallon salt-glazed crock August wanted.

"If you don't sell it, stop by the house and maybe I'll have something you want," August told him.

"You've got money now, August. I'll take money, mind you."

"No, I won't give money for crockery," August said.

"Well, why is that?" the potter said. "People seem to think I want to trade only for merchandise."

"Well, it's merchandise you're making. It won't breed, will it?"

"You sold in the outlands for money, didn't you?"

"Yes, but this isn't the outlands up here," August said.

How strange it was to see the potter become upset over so well established a system of trading. August knew a man named Caesar Cummings who year by year, because of his bride, spent all his cash money on her clothes and other dormant goods, instead of buying breeding stock, which would have the next year returned their cost to him and would have in years to come yielded a profit; he chose to buy clothes and trinkets for this pretty woman, and he lived in poverty. They were perhaps happy, even so; he had heard they were happy, contented people.

"Am I to drive all this lame stock up to your place, to see if you've got a piece of leather I can use?" the potter said.

"No, no," August said, trying to placate him, and began commenting on the breezy, sunny weather, all the while moving away from him, for the potter appeared to be angry. Potters were irrational about business matters, at best. No telling what a potter would do under stress. "Maybe you'll capture that there girl," he called back to him.

I could have captured her myself, he thought as he walked along. My conscience got in the way. Though I never could harm any creature, and I don't have to stoop to traffic in blacks. Last year I put my money into heifers, and as a consequence this year I was able to drive cattle as well as pigs to market and to recover my money, which I have put into a Jersey cow and a red boar. Next year I will, therefore, have better pigs to sell, as well as a calf to sell, as well as my beef cattle to sell, and I will get my money back, my cash money, which I will buy more heifers with, or maybe horses. Each year, more and more, year by year, I can build my fortune in an orderly way.

Of course, I ought to marry, he thought, I really ought to get that deed done. It's lonely living with Sarah's ghost. I need a woman close to hand. And I will need help to drive so much stock to market. This year I hired two boys for part of the way to town, but that is expensive. I need a strong wife, and as soon as nature will provide them, I need strong children.

The Wright daughter, Ama, she is strong. She is modest and is mildly pretty. She appears to be healthy. Her dowry will be substantial, too.

So he thought, comforting himself with his everyday sort of plans, as he moved along.

Twilight. The prettiest time of the day. He had told Sarah they should face their house toward the west, so they could sit at the fireplace and look out the door and see the sun set. They did place it just that way, too, and many a night he would come in from work in time to eat his supper as the sun went down. His soul was fed the same time his stomach was. Often as not, all he was eating was cornbread and buttermilk, but he was looking at a feast laid in a great hall, one of pheasants and partridges and cold turkeys and roasted ducks and sausages and fruit, sweet sweaty fruit dangling to be picked before it fell—fell forever through the air.

Twilight was the time to prepare a camp for the night, for darkness would settle fast in the mountains, especially in deep woods, but a man alone must be careful of his company. He ought to stay with those he knows. August hoped to come across somebody from his own community, preferably a family, for he didn't care as much for the conversation of a man as he did for that of a woman and her children; men wanted to talk about hunting and politics and moving to the west someday, such uprooting thoughts, and women and children wanted to talk about what they are doing, the firemaking, the cooking, the funny shape of a rock they've found, the path to the spring, whether the water is too cold, which way the wind is blowing, what they are cooking for supper, what they will have for breakfast, where everybody will sleep, what if it rains. He preferred such practical conversation, for the ideas didn't take him out of his own body and sail him off into purposes which had no basis in his own reality, no place in his plans. A woman's conversation was better to keep company with.

He passed several small camps where he was invited to stop. Most all people on the road were friendly, even though they also were guarded of strangers. They first would ask his name and where he was from. His name was recognized by several of them, for when Sarah fell her death was a matter of conversation in many communities. Also everybody knew of Harristown, and that it was a well-managed community, one whose citizens could be trusted.

"Stay with me," the men told him.

"Won't you at least eat with us?" the women said.

"How's Mooney doing up your way?" the men asked. "How much is land?"

But he went on, seeking somebody he knew, and to whom he could talk without confusion.

Until finally it was so dark the boar became reluctant to go any farther, so August put him in the cart, which caused the geese to deliver a burst of noisy advice. The cow mooed mournfully. "If your bag was dragging the ground, I would be more concerned," he told her. "Instead, you're carrying about a quart."

From the crest of the ridge, off to the west he could see God's dinner waiting for him, with a cloth made by a hundred ladies working half a century or so. Exquisite needlework.

Not much of a moon, he noticed, the more's the pity.

Darker and darker, this road. Too cold up here. The shifty limbs above him waved in worry. Darkness settled in. The blanched moonlight seemed to hollow every rut along the road, to contort every bush into weird beings dangerous to him. He hurried along, clutching his coat closer, sniffing suspiciously of the risky night.

A light up ahead. A fire burning on the road itself.

"Thank you, God, thank you, Sarah," he said, and hurried toward it, glad at last to be out of the darkness, calling out before him even as he arrived. And so in that boisterous way he entered Olaf Singleterry's camp.

5 THE BLACK GIRL was not yet found. He knew this at once because of the faces of the Negroes as they hurried toward him. "Did you find her?" one said. When he said no, he had not found her, they smiled nervously and turned away quickly.

"Many out looking for her?" August asked, watching them speculatively.

"He's got everybody looking. Has everybody messaging and looking," a young Negro said.

"That young buck, did they find him either?"

"No, no."

"Why don't you run off?" August asked the old man.

The Negro turned away suddenly, laughing from embarrassment. "And leave my friends?" he said.

The remark lingered in August's mind, for he had not expected it. A strange man, he thought; everyone is different and complicated.

At the fire August saw the bulky body of the master of them all, sitting squarely on the ground, his legs spread out in front of him, a tin pan on the ground before him, a wooden spoon in his hand; he was beating routinely on the pan while he gazed at the fire, into the golden flames and the white smoke.

August walked closer to him, attracted to him as a moth is to light. Glistening sweat was on his forehead and neck, even his shoulders were damp; his mouth was open, formed in a soundless "O." August crouched near him and stared into his face, at the two pimples on his lip, the thick patch of enlarged pores alongside his nose, the wad of spittle at the corner of his mouth.

Olaf was beating on the tin pan hypnotically, but he stopped, his hand in mid-air, the spoon poised, held waiting. "How you?" he said, his tongue thick. "What you here for? You find her?"

"No," August said.

"You following me?"

"No."

"No, it's not true," Olaf said, agreeing, though to what August didn't know. He tossed the spoon to the ground and awkwardly picked up a mug and drank from it. He drank deeply before he plopped the mug back onto the ground. He cursed the ground, then wiped his mouth with his hand, felt of his mouth, pressed his lips into a rosebud shape by his thumb and forefinger.

A baby was squalling in one of the covered wagons nearby.

"What you beating that pan for?" August said.

He moaned, ignoring him.

"You didn't catch them yet, did you?" August said.

"There have been three reports today of sightings. Tomorrow we'll catch them. Ah, God knows, she's not far away," Olaf said. He belched, a slobbery blurb from deep inside himself, then suddenly looked directly at August, intently tried to focus on him. "When she was born, instead of putting her out to wet nursing, I said, 'Go on, go on.' So her mama fed her herself. She fed her and cooked for us, too."

"So the girl lived near you?"

"I told you she did. Even as a baby she slept in my house. But I said oh no, it's not room in there for all this tribe, so I built her and her mama a little, a little—a little—" his fingers had found the place in his hair he wanted to scratch, found it after searching around "—a little room." He belched. "You know a planter never does anything; he has it all done, and when he says I plowed today, I cut hay, I fed the stock this evening, I slaughtered twelve hogs Saturday, I built a little room, why, he never did a thing, you see. Do you understand?"

"Yes, I do," August said.

"I didn't do it. You understand?"

"Yes."

" 'Cause I've got so much help I don't have time to do anything except tend to it. I was wondering last week what all my help does, and I decided what they do is feed each other."

"You hear it?" August asked him.

"Hear it?" he said.

"That squalling. A baby," he said, "way out here."

"Being born," Olaf said, nodding. He rubbed his nose with the flat of his hand, looking around for his spoon, failing to find it even though it lay close by. "I been beckoning it to be born with this here pan. I expect in Africa they would beat on a drum, but I don't have ary drum." He shouted toward one of the nearer wagons. "Well, has it tore loose from her yet?"

"It's born," somebody said at once.

"Well, let me see it then."

The old Negro man appeared out of the recesses of the camp and approached, walking carefully, bent and warped. In his two outstretched hands was the naked body of a newborn baby.

"What kind is it?" Olaf asked him gruffly, looking for his spoon. He saw it and stretched to retrieve it, trying while doing so not to lose his balance. "What?"

"A boy," the Negro said.

Olaf struck the pan a mighty blow. "Has its peter risen yet?"

"Not yet," the old Negro said solemnly.

"Well, it will," he said, and he glanced knowingly at August and winked. "They do rise, God knows, from morning to night. I mean from night to morning. Either way," he said, and laughed, coughing finally. "By the paths, by the mulberry trees, even in the river, so help me, in the water. It rises even in a snow," he said. "You know about buck blacks?"

"I don't know any blacks personally," August said.

"You're the world's luckiest man," Olaf said, "for they steal your time, your mind, your work, your blood, they bleed you dry." Angrily he struck the pan, this time with his hand, knocking the pan aside.

The old Negro came still closer, the babe held out before him. "Five fingers, five toes," he said.

"Ought to have ten," Olaf said grumpily, not looking at the child even yet.

"Has ten," the Negro said. He held the baby closer; the firelight played on its shiny skin.

A quiver came to Olaf's fat cheeks. "What color is it?" He had not looked at it.

"No need to worry 'bout that," the Negro said, almost sighing.

"No?" Olaf rubbed his eyes with his fat knuckles. He turned somewhat grandly and looked frankly, bluntly at the baby. "Oh, yes, he's brown enough to keep," he said.

August gasped aloud, jolted by the thought. "To keep?" he said.

"You want to say welcome to him, to this old world?" the Negro said.

Olaf took the baby in his hands, smiling at it, but at once the baby, as if sensing a lifetime awkwardness, began to squall.

"I never hurt him, did I?" Olaf said helplessly. He got to his feet, almost falling sideways, and stood hovering over the fire, staring strangely, perplexedly at the little creature in his hands, shaking it now and then, trying by that way to stop its sounds.

"Let me see how heavy it is," August said, offering to take it from him, afraid he would drop it or even throw it away, toss it into the flames.

Olaf pulled away, stumbled back from the fire, turned into the side of one of his wagons, tried to walk through it, found himself entangled with its canvas cover and ropes. The baby was bawling furiously. Olaf left the baby in the cover, upside down. It lay there bawling, its foot entangled in a rope, the firelight glistening on it. Maybe both feet were entangled in the ropes, or in a loop. Even Olaf was affected by the sight, for he crumpled to the ground before it, staring at the open, squalling mouth of his latest possession, at its firelighted chest and face.

The old Negro, standing off to one side, was solemn as ever, austere as ever, as if he had not noticed anything untoward.

"Look at it, look at it," Olaf said, whispering huskily, waving at August to come see it closer, to see it from where he saw it. "Ayyyyyy, God," he cried out. "Yeeeeee. Look at him, like a picture on a wall."

"Olaf, the world is crazy enough, even for a grown person," August said.

"Ayyyyyy, yeeeeee."

"Tell me what his name is," August said, trying desperately to distract him from the brutal sight, which had so utterly infatuated him. "What is his name?—tell me."

Olaf turned to August critically, irritated to be interrupted. "What's your name?" he said.

"August King."

"His name is King August," he said.

August laughed, more from surprise than good humor. "Clever," he said and nodded to the old Negro prompting him to get the baby. "That's a good name for him, Olaf," he said, trying to hold Olaf's attention.

The Negro moved gracefully, quickly, and removed the baby from the canvas, then holding it by its legs, the babe still upside down, he carried it away, as formal in manner as if removing from a banquet table an offending turkey. The squalling faded into the bosom of the camp, then stopped entirely, and August had a vision of a nipple being put into the baby's mouth.

In the abrupt ensuing silence August thought he heard the old Negro say, "King August is his name."

Olaf drank from the mug, drained the last drop of cider from it. He wiped his mouth with the sleeve of his shirt, then threw the mug at the pan he had been beating on, struck the pan squarely, a clattering, near deafening, clanging blow. The camp instantly was called to attention: dogs began barking, the baby began bawling, blacks began running back and forth, all without order or purpose. The pan had frightened everyone into believing that an angry judgment was about to be made about his work, so everybody was busy all of a sudden; empty pots were carried from one place to another, wagons were moved, horses were unhitched. Fleetingly appearing at the hooped opening of a big wagon was the baby, held in the arms of its mother, a woman with startlingly large black eyes, much like the girl's, with a bony face like the girl's, and on her face just now rested a look of benign beneficence.

"I'll be getting on," August said to Olaf, the remark surprising him, for he had not realized he was leaving. The awareness that he would not spend the night here, would not trust the place or himself to it, had come on him so gradually that he had not been conscious of it, or of its arrival.

"Well, do as you please," Olaf said grumpily.

The dogs were further excited by the movement of August's cart and stock. They snapped at his cow and barked at the red boar, but the little troop got out of camp without delay and the horse found the way along the dark road. August held to her bridle, for he couldn't see, now and then stumbling on rocks or ruts. "Keep going," he told her, "dear girl, keep going."

He stopped only when he no longer could hear the baby crying.

Why did he feel safer in the dark, stumbling about on the beast- and thief-ridden road, he asked himself, than in a camp, in Olaf's camp, well protected by dogs and fires?

There is something honest about a thief or a beast, he decided. They are what they admit to being, whereas Olaf is not honest, is not even predictable.

As a little boy August recalled saying to his mother— a sweet woman, somewhat shy, for she was always in the shadow of his father, himself an injured man born with a twisted right hand which in turn afflicted a hidden area of his being and made him sometimes shout out in anger, especially at wealthy men and healthy men—as a little boy August said to his mother, "How do you wrestle with a bear?" And she said, "Why, you grab it wherever you can."

But how do you wrestle with a disease of the soul? he wondered now. Where can it be grabbed? How can a man lie down to sleep in a camp where danger and despair fill the air?

He used one of his few matches to make a fire. To-morrow night when he reached Harristown he would need to use another one. Lord knows, he wanted to be home again; even the thought of being home rejuvenated him. He wanted to be there and see the room he had made and be with his own things again, and be free of the road entirely. To be home where everything was known and understood and expected, yet was interesting, where he was not under the shadow to prove himself in some new way, as he had been this morning.

He had to laugh, thinking about it, the absurdity of this morning. All that cornbread.

Soon the fire was flaring brightly. He crouched close to it and let its smoky warmth cover him. When he felt toasted and warm he led his cow close to the fire and milked her, catching the milk in a tin pot. "You'll go into a pasture day after tomorrow," he told her, speaking kindly to her. "I know you're unaccustomed to any such journey as this one. I understand."

In the firelight he gathered handfuls of acorns and chestnuts for the boar. He fed a few chestnuts to the horse, too. "I'm sorry to have so little for you," he told them. "This feed is only a promise of tomorrow night, when I will have you home and can feed you properly."

The horse stomped the ground impatiently. August broke one of his two cakes of cornbread and fed half of it to her. He fed a quarter of it to the boar, a quarter of it to the cow, and the specks left over, the crumbs, went to the geese.

He took the other loaf to his fire, where he set it beside the pot of milk. He could crumble some of the bread into the milk and let it soften. He would eat it that way, like his mother had when she had no teeth left and needed her bread softened. And he would fry a few rashers of bacon; he had a slab of bacon left in a sack in the cart.

He got it from the cart and also got the other pan, the lesser one, and set it on two fire-rocks. You have hen eggs in the wagon, August, he reminded himself. I believe you have two.

Well, I will save them for breakfast, he decided.

Lazily he watched the fire, vaguely worrying about the webby thoughts in his mind. I have shown you, Sarah, he thought. I have shown myself, too. I have today paid off the debt and have the papers signed. What you said was more than we could do, we have finished it today. I am satisfied with it.

"What's the matter?" he said to the boar, which was looking off toward the west woods, pawing the ground. "Some beasts out there?"

The wind is from the east, yet he watches the west, August noticed.

"Did you hear something?" he said to him.

The boar continued to thump the ground, and August thought, Yes, a wild beast is honest, but it honestly will tear you apart, too, and have an honest dinner of you, if you don't mind. "A thief in there?" he asked the boar.

He knew there was not, and a beast would not attack his fire. Even so, he couldn't eat his supper in comfort while having such lingering dreads, so he took from his pocket the money he had left and counted it in such a way that a thief would see it, then he put it in his coat in his cart and strolled over to the east woods, telling his horse he would try to find him some chestnuts. He went into the woods singing a song about Black Jack Davie. He sang his way into the woods, then quietly returned to wait in the bushes to see if a beast or thief appeared. He waited, shivering in the cold wind.

Directly, to his astonishment, he saw a movement on the other edge of the road. Breathlessly he watched as a slight, hesitant thief crept out of the bushes and approached the cart, then without stopping came on to

the fire and snatched up the bacon in the pan, splattering hot grease everywhere, then grabbed up the whole
loaf of cornbread—

"No, you don't either," August said, moving out onto
the road, hurling himself furiously forward, grabbing
the bread even as he fell to the ground, grappling for
it, the thief on the ground too—

It was the girl. Nothing in the world but the girl.
They were there on the road together.

6 HE CRAWLED over to the fire, which had been damaged by the scuffle, and began to build it back again. He watched her, fascinated by her, seeing her close to him again, pleased, although he shivered at each thought of his predicament.

She moaned and began to rub her ribs, where he had bruised her. She kept glancing at him, but not with fierceness. She was a woebegone, frightened girl with road dirt on her face and legs, her clothes torn, her cut, bruised body quaking from cold and misery.

"I'm starved," she said, her voice husky, quivering from the cold air and her own misery.

"Left you a pone of bread a foot wide this morning," he said.

She clutched her body with her thin arms.

"Ahhhhhh, Lord," he said, remembering the dogs.

"I was going up the path after you, to as't you to he'p me if you wouldn't mind, as't you again, even though you said the first time no you wouldn't he'p me."

He had never heard her talk so much, and he was fascinated by the low tremor in her voice, a persistent

moan which he supposed arose long ago in her ances-
try, a haunting sound from some other country.

"One was close enough to slobber on me, but his nose
was onto the bread by then," she said.

The bacon pan was lying on its face and had dirt
splattered inside it. He wiped it clean as he could with
his hand. The cornbread was on the road. He broke off
a piece and tossed it to her.

She ate it in one gulp.

"Ah, did you do that?" he said, astonished. "Now
listen here—" He broke off another piece and tossed it
to her.

She ate it in one gulp.

"Ah, law," he said, "your mama never teach you to
chew?"

"I've tried not to die all day. I ate leaves this morning
and they went through me like a fire."

"They cleaned you out, did they?"

"Made me so weak I've about died ever step of the
way, and they've scorched me with rash inside and out.
I've had to stop at ever rock and bush, seems like."

"Your fat owner is camped back that way. I can show
you, if you've had enough of freedom."

She considered that. "What's he a-doing?"

"He'll ride you home in a carriage, I expect, since he
seems to be so fond of you."

"What's he a-doing? I as't you."

"Exhibiting his new baby on a wagon."

"What baby?"

"That little baby some woman bore tonight."

"She never. She never bore yet. Not time."

"She bore tonight."

"It takes a twelve-month year."

He laughed, and that irritated her, but he didn't mind. "Ah, Lord knows. Who is the mother, do you know?"

"What it was, the baby?" she asked.

"A boy. One brown enough for him to keep, so you can stop worrying. What does he do with the white ones?"

She rested back on stiffened arms and watched him, studied him critically. She grunted finally and turned away.

"Is she your mama?"

She belched, and her stomach began growling. "I reckon she is." Her body was in distress obviously. She rubbed her cut arm across her face; it had been opened in several places by briers and rocks. "I'll eat most anything," she said.

"That's all I've got," he said, "most anything."

Suddenly she said to him, as if it were a new thought, "I'm not ever going back to him if I can he'p it. There's more to see in this life than his back yard. And I'd rather have all the fears of this jungle than the ones from his moods, for he changes fast as a cat on wet stones."

"Well, I'll feed you then," he said. "You can take this pot to the cart and put in it a handful each of sugar and flour, and bring me those two eggs." My Lord, she can talk, he thought. It's like an old song.

When she returned, he saw she had got more flour and sugar than he had asked for, but he said nothing about it. That was probably just as well. She stood nearby licking her hands clean—stood there in the

69

firelight licking her palms and between her fingers, like a young animal.

He broke the eggs into the flour and sugar, then stirred the mixture with a stick. He poured in enough of the milk to make a soft dough. Her stomach was grumbling and complaining, and she got the hiccups, so she was very much like a kettle that kept making noises and burps and comments and objections, though she didn't appear to notice any of them. She was attentive only to every move he made.

"He can't even butter his toast, 'less I help him, much less cook," she told him.

She must mean Olaf, he decided. Would she not call him simply he? Would there be need of another name on a plantation such as his, where he was lord and master and owner of everything and everybody. *He* said. *He* did. *He* won't allow. *He* agrees. *He* is angry. *He* is smiling. *He* hurt his foot. *He* won't eat just now. *He* says to make the fire or not to make the fire in the parlor or the bedroom, or to use more oak and less pine, or to plow the lower field, or that *he* won't allow you, nigger, to touch that carriage of his. *He* is God. Is there a higher God? Ask him. *He* is the one who would know.

"He was sick when I was a little girl age of seven and five months," she said, "and he lay in the bed four months, like a Turk, his head wrapped with cloths smelling of herbs and bark, and I would take him a root tea my mama made, take him tea and his eggs, which is all he ever wanted, that and mother's milk. He never even rolled over without help."

"Mother's milk?" August said, astounded.

"He sent a rider for it all the way to Burnsville and back ever day."

"Who milked it?" he said.

"Why, I never as't," she said. "I suppose the mother did it to her ownself."

"I never heard of anything like that," he said, embarrassed, and began stirring the fire. "I've heard of sick people drinking only goat's milk, but never—"

"He wouldn't think of cooking for hisself, let me tell you that."

"Here, drink all of it," he said, giving her the pot of milk. "Every drop," he said.

She drained it dry without pausing and obediently handed the pot back to him.

He sliced bacon into it. "You've had a full life, seems to me, buttering his toast and fetching mother's milk for him," he said.

"Mama he'ped him use the pan. I refused to do it, but I he'ped him in most ever other way. I used to stan' by his bed with spring water in a pail and wet his cloths and listen to him moan and pray and grind his teeth and curse his mama, who died twenty-one years ago on the side of the hill of a heart break, and one night when I was twelve years four months I sat there all night thinkin' he would die most any time, kept pressing his hand and as'tin' first one spirit then another to he'p him, calling on all the lords I ever heard of, and next morning he felt so much better he gave me the credit for it and tol' me ever night to sleep on the mat aside his bed, and after that he almost always had me as close to him as his han'. Even when he went to ride I rode on a pony thirteen han's high, which he said I could own, but when I was fourteen years three months he up and sold it because I spit at him."

"You spit at him?"

"At his face."

"The pony?"

"No. The man."

"You did not, surely."

"I spit at him four diff'rent times."

"Why?"

"He laughed at me because this boy Hal like me, and he found us in swimming in the river together and he told me he would beat Hal or sell him off, one or the other, as I decided. He had stood in a thicket watching us all the while."

"What did you choose?"

"I spit at him is all I could do. I've never felt more he'pless in my life. Standing in a thicket, and him grown. So he sold my pony."

"And sold your friend, too?"

"Sold them both to the same man," she said, a husky whisper, her voice dropping so low he could scarcely hear her.

"I'm sorry," he said, awkwardly embarrassed.

He put the cooked bacon on a rock and poured into the same pan enough dough to make a thin pancake. At once it began to sputter and bake. When he finished browning it, he sprinkled bacon crumbs over the top, then folded the pancake over the bacon.

The girl was astonished by all this and watched it, sighing and moaning in awe of it. When he offered her the pancake, she hesitated for the briefest moment to accept it, then she took it and stuffed it into her mouth, hot as it was, all of, every bit of it, and swallowed it all.

"Ah, stop that," he said. "You ought to be whipped, is my opinion. Here I cook you something good, and you treat it like a leftover rind."

She sat there studying him, confused, hurt by his anger.

"You eat very much like a dog I knew once," he told her.

"You min' your ownself," she said angrily, yet ashamed, too. "I don't tell you how to eat."

"Well, I wish you would. I certainly wish you would. We could have an evening's entertainment from the instructions. Tell me what you know about it."

She glared at him, embarrassed yet defiant.

He poured another pancake into the pan and while it browned got his jug of brandy from the cart and took a swallow of it. "I need strengthening if I'm going to have to train you. And I need warming, too. It's cold up here on this ridge, you know it, colder than I remember it being last year, but the air is dry and sprightly, there's no sickness in it."

She sniffed at the jug.

"What do you think of it?" he said.

She wrinkled her nose, as if the smell offended her. "It's not cider."

"I've not got room in a cart to haul cider," he said. "Here, cup your hands."

"He never allowed me any, said Indians and niggers shouldn't have it."

"Here, hold them out, I tell you. You do what I say now, not him."

She did so obediently.

He poured an ounce or two of the brandy into her hands. "Drink it," he said.

She sucked it into her mouth all at one gasp and when it burned her she began to grimace in distress. "Ahhhhhh," she said, coughing, trying to speak. "Youuuuuuuu—" she began, her mouth unable to let go of the word.

"Burn you?" he said, as if he were surprised by it. "Well, you shouldn't have drunk it all in a moment."

"Burned me," she admitted huskily.

"Here," he said, offering her another drink, "hold out your hands."

She glared at him. "No, I'll not."

"Lick it slowly. Hold out your hands, I say."

She did as he instructed and this time slowly sucked the drink into her mouth, none too pleased with it, especially at first, he attentive to the ever-changing expressions of pain and pleasure, and her groans and grunts and other noises of opinion. It was a pleasure to watch her and listen to her, to try to think up ways to arouse and please her, a half-naked nut-brown waif trained to do as she was told, a friendly, bug-bitten, brier-scratched, bowel-distressed young pet, especially pretty now with the firelight on her, flickering over her brown skin and torn dress, particularly attractive to him, appealing to him now because of his loneliness, or maybe because of her need of him, dependency on him. "You crept through the woods all day, following me, didn't you?" he said.

"Been exploring along the way," she said, "your cart's so slow."

He got from the cart a pocketful of sugar and sprinkled some of that on her damp palms. She sat at the fire licking her hands like a kitten licks its paws, gasping and moaning with pleasure. To him it was a sensual performance, and his old desires, buried in the graves up back of his house, were aroused by this brown young animal with stomach and bowel pains.

This time when the pancake was brown, he splashed brandy into the pan and let it catch fire, which surprised her, which amused her too.

"I allow," she said.

When the fire went out, he sprinkled sugar on the pancake and rolled it up. He was bound and determined to impress her, since she was so appreciative. "My mama did it this way on occasions," he told her.

"I never saw anybody burn water afore," she said.

He offered it to her, reminding her to take care. She took the pancake in both hands, then with a quick, knowing glance she began to munch at one end of it, one bite at a time. As he watched her she took other bites and chewed them. When she swallowed the last one, she looked over at him and laughed, the first time he had heard her laugh, a sudden, delighted series of sounds, as if amusement at herself had become too much for her any longer to contain.

"Those rock cuts hurt you?" he asked her.

"They do," she said, "once I stop walkin'."

"You must have walked in many a dangerous place."

"Through laurel slicks so thick not even a snake would go through, but there was no way 'round them."

"You want me to doctor those feet for you?"

She nodded, then sat waiting for him to tell her what to do.

"It's an old cure," he said. He swished brandy in his mouth, then leaned over her leg and spit it on her feet.

It burned sharply, and she pulled herself away from him, pushed herself, wriggling across the ground, gasping. She stationed herself a fair distance from him, glaring at him fiercely.

"It's for your own good," he said, surprised by the sudden flurry. "It didn't hurt all that much surely."

"I don't want any more of it."

"Well, all right," he said. "But it was for your own good, believe me."

She crawled to the far side of the fire from him and huddled there, her arms clutching her body for warmth and protection, her dark gaze resting from time to time on him, wondering about him, testing him, testing her knowledge of him, of the two of them alone on this remote place on the road.

Of course, he had known the brandy would sting her. He knew he should have warned her. Sometimes the devil gets into me that way, he thought, and it seems like there's nothing I can do about it.

"My wife Sarah once was given an orange by our neighbor, the German, for Christmas," he said.

The girl poked the fire with a stick and blew on it. "An orange for her ownself?"

"He used to come up to my house, said he came by to see could he help me, but it got so ever time I returned home from work or from the mill he was there with her. I never distrusted Sarah, for once she gave her word she was steady by it. But I never trusted him one bit. He might do most anything merely for the experience of it. Why he gave her a gift at all, I don't know."

"What went with the orange?"

"I'm telling you. She cooked it."

The girl's eyes flashed at him. "Why, she never. If I had an orange, last thing I'd do—"

"If you had an orange, you'd swallow it whole, peels and all," he said.

"I wouldn't cook it, I'll say that."

"She peeled it and cut the peelings up, then she took the sections of the orange apart, then she said if I would kill her a chicken she would cook it, too. What you scratching those bites for? You'll get them to festering."

She accepted that opinion with the same critical skepticism she had for Sarah's recipe, but she did stop scratching the bites.

"It was a Saturday and she was planning this hen for Sunday dinner, don't you know? Usually on Sunday we go to church, the two of us; it's about a ten-minute walk away. If we don't have a preacher, one of the leaders will speak. For instance, Mr. Wright will speak to the congregation about farming. He believes in a three-year rotation system. He talks about it as if God does, too." He laughed, but she didn't seem to understand. "Or somebody else will speak—and you might find this surprising—I've spoken there myself."

"You a preacher?" She was openly suspicious of the idea.

"A few months ago the congregation put me on the Board on nomination of Mr. Wright, and as a member of the Board I was asked to take one Sunday of it and try to swing the ax for them, which scared me to death, I admit. I never slept one whole night through. But I got up before the congregation, which numbers almost a hundred people, not counting children, and asked the other leaders what to sing, and they agreed on a selection, so I lined that song out. I can't sing well, but I did my best. I fought it through, I quavered at it."

"Well, are you tellin' about your wife's orange, or not?" she said.

"Spoke on Infant Baptism. I came out for it." He

laughed at his own joke, but again she didn't respond; she was a dour little girl, just now, somewhat haunting in the way she looked at him, and even the way she bent over the fire, glancing now and then at him, unsure of him or unsure of herself with him. "Preachers have all manner of powers, they tell me," she said.

"I preached on the baptismal water being the same as what gushed from Jesus' side when the Roman soldier speared him on Mount Golgotha. I read that as a boy in a book. I said the water in the river that we baptize with, that's Jesus' blood from his side."

"Why, it's not," she said.

He looked up at her, astonished. "I read it, I tell you, as a boy. What do you know about doctrine?"

"I know about river water," she said.

"Doctrine is not river water. It's beyond us both."

"Well, upon my word," she said, and went to poking at the fire, giving him an occasional critical glance. "Did she cook that orange or not?"

"I'm telling about it as plain as I can. She said to me she wasn't going to be able to go to church with me because of this chicken. I asked her about it, said at least to come and visit with everybody. Sunday's the only time we have to visit with everybody, as you know."

"I never go to church," she said.

"Why, you should," he said.

"He won't let any of us go."

"Who? Who is he to deny you the word of God?"

"We can go among ourselves, but we have nobody who can read."

"What about that old white-haired, stumpy man?"

"He acts like he can. He'll stan' up front of us with the

book open in his han', but what he says is what he wants us to hear, bein' obedient to our master, and such as that."

"That's in the Bible, I'll admit," he said.

"Not on ever page, it's not. We had a man name of Bath who could read, and he said it was seldom mentioned. He was sold to Mississippi."

"I thought all the blacks at Hobbs have a common service, where they sing and worship together."

"He won't let us go to it. He's 'fraid we'll get ideas or diseases from the other niggers." She looked up at him, her big black eyes shining. "A white preacher came to our place, to our farm once, but I wouldn't go to hear him."

"Wouldn't trust him?" August said.

"No, I wouldn't," she said.

"Do you trust any white man?" he said.

She answered directly, not in anger but as a matter of truth. "No, no," she said. "The only ones I ever have known keep changing ever day."

He roused himself, stood up, stretched. "Anyway, I said to Sarah, 'Come to church with me whatever else you do,' but Sarah said no, that she had this idea about cooking the chicken and to bring the German and his wife home with me, and even their children if necessary. I said, 'Well, no, I'll not.' I mean, it wasn't necessary to have the German at my house all the time. I said, 'Look here, I have for a year got seeds for that hen to eat, have rocked and logged up the chicken house so the possums and foxes wouldn't get her, and the German has done nothing at all.' But Sarah insisted that I invite him and his wife. She said she had this fine idea

79

about how to cook this chicken. And I said, 'When are you going to eat your orange that the German gave you?' And she said, 'I'm going to cook it inside the chicken.' "

The girl stared at him. "Why, she never."

"It's the truth, so help me."

"Why, she never, unless'n she was crazy."

The girl was a wonder to see. Her big eyes were round as saucers, and her mouth was open in astonishment. She was a fine audience, that was the truth of it; she was full of astonishments and concentration. He poured her a bit more brandy as a reward for her interest, and took some himself. She seemed to be hoping for sugar, too, so he sugared her palm for her.

"I said, 'No, you're not going to cook it either.' It wasn't often I ordered Sarah, especially during this period when she was mourning over our baby, but I've always liked baked chicken as well as any food in the world, and I had got jealous of the German, I admit it, for seemed like Sarah was turning in her grief more to him than to me—"

"Well, did she cook the orange?" she said.

"I can eat an orange or leave it alone myself, it's a foreign fruit to me; I didn't grow up on oranges and rarely tasted one before I was nineteen, and that one had to be shared with two brothers and two sisters. I like an orange, mind you, but I like it to itself. I never thought of an orange being mixed with anything else, much less baked. I said, 'No, you're not, Sarah.' She didn't argue, but she grew sullen and closed up on me—"

"Sullen?"

"So I went on to church, and—listen to this—after church the German asked me if he could come to dinner with me."

"Why, law," she said, surprised. "He knew it all the while."

"He said nothing about his children coming, too, thank the Lord. I said, yes, yes, by all means. Seems like I always fold up scared before him, he always has so much confidence. We three walked up to the house through the snow, his wife Mina with us, stopping now and then on the little climb to rest our lungs, for it was wintertime, remember, and the air was cold and searing, and I said to them, 'We have a chicken for dinner, I believe,' and he said, 'That's true,' which irritated me, to think he knew. How did he know? And I said, 'But I told her not to cook the orange with it,' and he turned on me irritably as if I didn't know my own house and said, 'Why did you do that?' And I said, 'How did you know about her orangy notion anyway?' And he muttered something strange and waved his arms, dismissing me, as he does when he's determined to avoid embarrassment. And his own wife Mina, who was studying the ground, never looked up; she felt that strange about it. I never doubted my wife Sarah for a second, as I said to you, but I didn't trust the German, don't you see? I would never think of abandoning a vow I made, and it was impossible for me to believe Sarah would either—a woman has more trouble that way than a man, don't they?"

She said nothing.

"When it comes to being unfaithful, I mean. Don't they?"

"You going to cook any more cakes?" she said.

He poured the last bit of dough into the pan and let it start to simmer, even as she sniffed and studied the pancake, and moistened her lips with her tongue.

"As I came into the yard, I smelled that cooked orange," he said.

"Well, I'm surprised she went on and cooked it," she said emphatically, "after what you told her."

"I was surprised. I'll admit that to you. Sarah had been obedient and considerate most of the time we had lived together, up until the baby's birth, then she seemed to shrivel up inside, get dry and brittle."

The girl stared at him, her lips pouting with her concern for him. "What you do?"

"I went up in the field to think it through," he said.

"Why," she said helplessly, "think it through?"

"And sat on a rock near my baby's grave and asked myself what I was going to do."

"As't yourself?" she said.

"I have found it most helpful at times to ask myself for my best advice. And to ask God."

"Oh, law," she said, a blank admission of her dismay, her disappointment in him.

"To tell God what burdens me. He has power to change it all, even to change that orangy dinner. God has the power to uncook that orange."

"Ahhh, he does not."

"Your denial is an outright defiance of doctrine. I have told you a great truth."

"Uncook an orange?"

"I'm telling you, whatever your name is—"

She moaned in misery and shook her head. "Not true. Can't uncook fruit."

"What is your name anyway?" he said, giving her the last pancake. "Did he name you?"

"He named me after a Virginia town when I was born. He was told I was a boy."

"So he named you what?"

"Williamsburg."

"Williamsburg. Oh, my Lord. Williamsburg. You're not supposed to be called William, much less Burg," he said. "Tell me again what he named you."

"I told you they thought—"

"Didn't they look to see what kind you were?"

"I don't know what they did, much less what they didn't do. I wasn't but half a day old." She was groveling in her embarrassment. "But I'm called Annalees by most ever one today, or Anna for the short of it."

"Who named you that?"

"I saw nobody else was goin' to do the least bit properly by me, so I name' myself."

"I prefer Annalees, I'll admit," he said.

She crawled a foot or two closer to him, around to the nearer side of the fire. "What you do," she said, "about that wife, once you'd prayed?"

"Well, I saw her come out into the yard and call for me, and I felt sorry for her."

"Sorry for her?" she said helplessly. "After her doing what you'd said not to do—"

"I let her call me many times, mind you, before I answered, but I did answer finally, for Sarah and I had for many years been close. I went down through the field, while she stood near the cabin corner waiting, not with her hands on her hips or in any way defiant, for she knew we had been friendly to one another, and I suspect she was concerned about what I would say, she not knowing, for she had obviously defied me outright, had made me seem unimportant in my own house. I knew what my father would have done—he would have shouted at her, he would have let her know his anguish, for anything fierce he needed to say was like the breaking of a boil inside his soul. There were never secrets about the way he felt. But my mama never in this world would have crossed him this way."

"What did you do to her?"

"I told her that she had missed a fine church service. Then I went into the house and sat down at the table. The three of them had already begun eating. The German had carved my chicken himself. He had a seepy grin on his face as he watched me, wondering if I would dare say something to spoil the meal. I served myself a piece of chicken. I took a drumstick, best I recall. From the carcass I gouged out some of the orange. The orange hadn't cooked into a pulp at all, but had its texture even yet; most of it had been inside the chicken. Sarah waited, amazed at me and no doubt surprised at herself. Everybody watched me."

"I imagine," Annalees said.

"I ate the drumstick and orange bits and looked up finally and said, 'Sarah, I find a chicken tastes good when it's cooked this way.'"

Annalees' mouth fell open. A groan came out of her. "Ahhhhh, no," she said, astounded. "You never," she said.

"I turned to the German's wife and I said, 'Mina, you like it all right?' And Mina smiled at me in a wistful way —she's the one that milks for me, now that I'm away, and straightens up my place—"

"You mean you never even, you never mention—angry with—that wife of yours?" Annalees was on her knees, staring at him.

"What you mean?" he said, trying to be clear and fair. "She knew I was furious with her, didn't she?"

"How she know?"

"I went up into the field, didn't I? And she heard me tell her not to cook it."

"I never heard such a kindly story in my life," she said furiously.

He was astonished at her. "You want me to beat her?"

"There's nothing to it," she said. "Why you tell a story like that?"

Finally he said, "All right, I don't want to hear any more about it."

She was putting small rocks into the brandy jug. One after another she dusted the rocks with her fingers, then blew on them, dropped them into the jug. How long she had done it before he noticed it, he had no idea, and even after he noticed it he was so fascinated by watching her that he said nothing to reprimand her. One little rock after another, her concentration solely on this activity, she scrounging around her to choose the best rock to contaminate his brandy with, cleaning it with her dirty hands, blowing her breath on it, dropping it into his brandy jug.

He suddenly slapped her hand back from the jug, struck it hard, and a gasp came out of her, a scowl came over her face.

"Stop that," he said.

She pouted like a child. "What?" she said, confused, even dismayed to be spoken to this way, so roughly. Her lips began to tremble and she was close to tears.

"Those rocks," he said.

She didn't seem to know what he meant.

A child, he thought. That's all she is. Playing a child's games.

"When Mr. Wright came up the road with that oldest son of his, I was breaking limbs for firewood," he said, talking along idly, as much to himself and the night as to her. "Never had he come up to my place before, even though I had been to his, had walked his daughter home from church a few times and had sat on his porch. He said to me, 'August, there's a problem down the river a mile in the Philip Smith house, and I want to ask for your view.' Why he had never asked my opinion before, so I knew then he was accepting me more and more into the community. This was before he ever even asked me to speak in church."

"What was the matter with Mr. Smith?" the girl said.

"Oh, something or other embarrassing. I don't know. The point is that Mr. Wright asked me, and I was so nervous I said to him, 'Well, what do you think I ought to say to you?'"

She stared at him, her head tilted to one side as if listening for some other sounds or words. "What was it he as't you?" she said.

"He was asking me for advice, and I was asking him to advise me about my advice, don't you understand? Later I thought how foolish I was."

"What was it he said, I wonder," she said.

"He said that the man ought to give up the girl, the one he had taken home with him in spite of being married to a woman his own age, about sixty, I suppose. He had children living there at the house who were older than the girl, who was only fifteen, sixteen, about your age, I expect."

A scowl came over her face, much as if night had suddenly settled in a place, and she shook her head irritably. "Don't want to hear," she said, and abruptly turned away.

"The girl's father lived in Burnsville, said he would rather kill her than have her back home, but Mr. Wright said no, we ought to insist he take her back and rear her baby, should she bear one. And I did hesitate to agree to that. Anything less would undermine the family and hurt the reputation of the church and the community, that's what Mr. Wright said, and so I said, 'Yes, yes,' for I wanted to agree with him. Everybody has to agree with Mr. Wright, for he has got the mind and the money in my part of the world, just as Olaf has it in yours."

Annalees wasn't listening any longer; for some reason she appeared to be upset because of the story.

"Mr. Wright used to come ask my opinion, maybe once a week after that, so in a few months others were asking me what I thought about matters, too, even asking if I would help them get Mooney to loan them money to buy more land, or hire a doctor, or send a son to school, or whatever it was. He controls most everything, Mooney Wright does, I tell you. You ever hear of him down your way?"

She shrugged, but said nothing.

"No, I suppose it's your man down there, that has the slaves."

Later she began quietly, absent-mindedly talking, he halfway listening to what she said, not understanding much of it. She was scratching bites on her legs as she talked to him, as she talked to herself really, her mind twisting its way through ideas much as her finger was finding its way through the dirt on the road before her, between her and the fire. ". . . which is the only time I ever saw her, with her thinking she was riding a horse and was thundering along the road toward the river, riding on her own pallet in her own room, her sister having done it to her . . ." And again, ". . . not that you should ever point to anybody with your dog finger, since that's the one you spell a person with. Even him. I've known niggers to try to spell him . . ." And again, ". . . so I thought why not go on down the road and be a free person, why not as stay here and watch his breathing and listen to him talk so big and see him kill my frog."

"Your frog?" August said.

"Which was all I had in the way of a pet to call my own, and I kept it with my mama and me in our room, but one evenin' at the fall of light when mama and me was cooking supper, was cooking pork ribs and sweet potatoes, not that he allowed us to eat them except what we stole for ourselves, licked off our own fingers, my frog got out the door and must have went past us and got into the room where the family was sitting down to wait for their food, and his wife let out a scream that broke a cup. Then he stomped it with his boot."

"Ahhhh, Lord knows. He's not much of a man, to stomp a frog."

"He drinks too much is one trouble about him, and he gets to feeling strong."

"Even so," he said, a laziness, a sleepiness coming over him now, for the day had been long and trying. "I wonder about tomorrow," he said. "What you planning to do?"

"Take a day at a time," she said. "Mama said to try to manage more'n one at a time give you too much sorrow and too much gladness, so take each day as it come."

"Yes," he said, "it sounds all right." What was he going to do with a child like this? "Stop scratching your legs," he told her.

Her lips began quivering. "Don't you talk like that to me," she said.

"All right," he said, not wanting to be unkind. "I don't know what I'm going to do with you. A man can get himself killed out on this road."

"What you mean?" she said.

"I suppose you wouldn't care what they do to me," he said.

She stared at him. "Do what to you?"

"Stop screwing your lips up like that. How old are you anyway?"

"Fifteen," she said.

"Shoot me. Hang me. Beat me up." The boar nearby was rooting into the road. "Stop that," he said irritably. And to the girl he said, "Stop scratching. Don't you have any modesty?" She was scratching her thighs, near her crotch. "You an animal?" he said.

Tears welled up into her eyes, but even so there was a toughness to her face; she was a competent little creature, a bundle of pride and feeling, accustomed to being buffeted and criticized, yet to holding her own.

"Just don't scratch so much," he said. She had absolutely no inhibitions that he could discover.

Yet look, just now, the way she turns her head, the proud way she holds her head, the way the golden firelight plays on her face, the sudden beauty that has settled on her, as if coming to her from a long way off, not born in her; rather she was born in it, a royalty, some distant nobility in her eyes, the tilt of the head. The long, slender, bony legs, one beautiful foot slowly moving in the dirt, soothing its own hurts and bruises . . .

". . . and his daughter died and we heard her voice, first one night and then another, him and me heard her voice calling, and she being only five years old but she had made her way back to him. Her and me had played most ever day together, and if she didn't do what I said to do, I would strike her down, and when she cried and her mama come, I would say she fell down and hurt her ownself. But I never wanted her dead."

"No, I guess not," he said lazily. Beautiful breasts, young breasts, one of them partially visible through a torn place on her dress. Ah, August, don't think such thoughts. "The devil, even up here on the road," he said.

"She cried in the night to us, but never moved a chair. Then one night she struck me when I lay asleep, and I woke crying, there near his bed. Her hand was outlined on my face for even as long as it took him to light a lantern to see by. And he said to me, 'Why, who would hate you, Annalees?' And I said, 'It was your own daughter done it.' And he said, 'Why, she's dead, and was only five years old.' And I said, 'She's seven year old, for she's been buried two year and a month.' "

August went to get wood for the fire. He would hear her talking, even as he broke off branches from the trees, branches that overhung the road, or broke off sticks of bushes; she was talking along as if he were still there. She doesn't talk to me at all, he thought; she talks to herself, to her ghosts and spirits, and to him, who is always in her mind.

"That horse he's got, that Virginia horse," he asked her, dumping wood on the fire, "is that a fair mount?"

"Why, he's got several. She used to fuss at him, complain, for whenever he went off on a journey he would come home with yet another horse. 'You can't ride but one,' she would say."

"That horse name of Samson Lee."

"She's hateful. But he doesn't care. He like horses with fire in them, he says."

"You have fire in you?" he asked.

"Law, yes," she said, and suddenly smiled at him.

"You not been broke, is that it?" he said.

"What you mean?" She rubbed her nose, then scratched a bug-bite on her chin. "You mean I scared? I must been scared of him, for when I woke up yesterday mornin' and saw the sky over me, no roof, none of his over me, no walls of his around me, I had the freest breath come in, and I felt so light I wanted to fly away."

How pretty her face just now, looking up at the treetops, as if she were ready to fly off into the sky somehow. An amazingly alert face, he thought, changing every now and then, often reflecting some new affection or interest or hate or fear or longing.

"Did she fall a long ways?" she asked suddenly.

"Who you mean?"

"That woman." She lay back on the ground and turned to the fire, which glowed on her skin. "Why she fall?" she said.

"I wish people wouldn't ask me that over and over," he said irritably. "Her shoe was quite faulty, I know that. When the men found the body, they found that her left shoe was faulty, as I told them they would, but she had never asked me to fix it. It had been faulty for some time, but she wouldn't ask anything of me or talk to me."

"Did you see her fall?"

"You mean did I see her trip and fall?"

"Did you see her falling?"

"No."

"I wonder how she fell," she said, "whether like a bird with her arms outstretched or bundled up. I would fall with my arms outstretched."

Cold the air around him and the thoughts in his mind, to hear so calmly mentioned the image of his wife in the air long worrying months ago. "I wish people wouldn't keep bringing up what I want to forget."

"But you never saw her."

"No. I didn't see her after she left my house that morning."

"Then what you need to forget? You can't forget what you never saw."

"Well, if that's not an extraordinary statement. I can certainly forget, I can try to forget what I never saw.

Why, what do you mean? Is the mind composed of pictures?"

"Were you mean to her?"

"I wish you would talk about yourself and let me alone."

"I was askin'—"

"Hush," he said abruptly. "Not a word."

She looked up at him, a tiny smile playing on her lips, for she had found a weak place in him. "You afraid?"

He struck her hip, slapped her hard. "Hush. Not another word. I have had eleven months of asking myself questions I can't answer, and I don't need any help with it. Not from any stinking nigger girl found free on the road."

The smile crumpled and a flash of hurt, of pain went over her face, then she laid her head forward on the ground, on her arm on the ground, and she moaned, a sad sound in the still night.

At once he felt sorry, both for her and for himself. He was subject, was a slave to his own irritability. He was abrupt with people often, once they began to pry into the secrets he carried. His life was a pack of secrets, held close and privately, and he could not abide anybody peering inside, including Sarah. Particularly Sarah. But why would he mind, he wondered, a girl like this asking his opinions?

He took a little piece of cornbread and doused it with brandy, then sprinkled it with sugar. He put one corner of the bread close to her mouth and let her bite off a bit of it. "You chew now," he told her.

She lay there chewing.

"No need to be disappointed with me," he said. "I'm

mostly little fits of opinion that don't amount to anything."

A long while he sat there, cold in his bones, staring before him at the nighttime road, listening to her breathe as she lay near him on the ground, thinking about Sarah, a chill of fear on him, a sweat on his face.

"I never have had anybody close to me die," she said.

"Your time will come for mourning. It comes to all of us."

"He sells them, once they get up in years. I mourn them then."

The fire had burned down. We need to build it up, he thought, if it is going to protect us from the beasts. "Though they are full of food now," he said aloud.

"Who?" she said.

"Most all of them," he said. "They have been fed well on this road."

"I've not, until tonight," she said.

I could break that branch off the tree, he thought, the one that hangs low near the cart. It's dead, I think.

"You going to he'p me tomorrow?" she said softly.

"Yes," he said.

"Why?"

"I knew it was so, that I would, once you asked me. I don't know why. I've never done anything like this before, you understand."

"What will they do to you, if you he'p me?"

"Why, I don't know," he said.

"They're so— I wonder what they would do with me, what they would do, all those men." Suddenly she said, "I'll jump off a cliff afore they catch me. I'll do what your wife did. I'll die falling with my arms outstretched,

I imagine. I'll not be caught, and I'll not go home. There's something better'n that."

"Hush, hush," he said, and tried to turn away from the thought of her dying, from thoughts of death at all. "You hush about her, you hear me?" he said.

He made room for her to lie down in the cart. The geese objected, and he couldn't rearrange the big bags of goods like he wanted to, for fear of their beaks and wings. The cart was less than four feet wide, but that was enough room for her, once she bent her legs and cuddled herself for the night. The sideboards were about a foot high, and so was the tailgate. "Tomorrow I'll leave that sugar and salt at the front opening and put the coffee and flour back here," he told her. Then she couldn't be seen, he imagined, unless a man on horseback came quite close. "You can hide in here very well tomorrow," he told her.

He stood at the cart listening to her breathe. Like Sarah, he thought, like most anybody trying to go to sleep, he imagined, heavier than normal breathing.

He put a few sticks on the fire and sat close to it, wondering about Sarah and where their lives had got lost from one another. He had come to love her sometime during their first year of marriage, and he had missed her if he didn't see her, even for half a day.

The forest sounds had reached their normal night-time level of bickering and singing. A wolf was now and then heard howling a long way off.

Nigger, nigger in the night—

What song was that from? Was it a song?

What a lean, handsome child she is, he thought. I

have no doubt Olaf wants her home again. Even if she were not his own daughter . . .

His mind got drowsy. Sleepy mind.

"Tomorrow, God, will we reach home?" he said. "I want so much for her to see my house."

What a peculiar need you express, August.

My room, my fire, my hiding places, my table, my chairs. To show her what I have made for her.

For her? he asked himself.

For Sarah. For my wife.

I want her to see what I have made to live in, to own, he thought.

My, my, but she owns nothing. Not even her torn dress is hers. You shouldn't concern yourself unduly about her, August.

I need someone just now, he thought.

August, you must be mature and sensible.

A light on the road. He lay talking, imagining he was talking to a light on the road, to a ball of fire on the road, to himself on the road.

> Nigger, nigger in the night,
> Do you see the world afire?
> Do you hear God crying?

Nigger, nigger in the night, do I see God's fire, can I see his face?

The promised land, after forty years in the wilderness.

The promised land is somewhere toward the north.

I want to sleep, he thought. As I fall asleep I must remain awake. I must be mindful to be up before dawn. We must be on the road by then, the girl well hid in the cart, so I must not trust to a deep sleep.

Will I help her, the girl? When did I decide to help her?

Into the ground I dug a hole. With my hands I pulled the rocks from the sides of the hole. I lifted them, rolled them. I stood in the mouth of the earth, the mouth of the body of my land of work and fear, my wife saying we could never do so much.

The earth had a red mouth, red gums; its teeth were rocks, glistening to bite me and my baby dressed in a white dress. I laid her in the spittle. Sarah stood above the mouth, a gaunt bird hovering. She had told me the child would not die, could not die, was not dead. "Even in this wild land to which you have brought me, I have cured her and she is not dead, I have saved her with my prayers and medicines."

Four days it lay dead in our bed. Only then did she not stop me when I went out to dig a mouth to eat it.

I stood amid the gums, the spittle of the mouth gleaming on the craggy teeth, sopping the white dress at my feet. I must cover her over.

But I could not watch myself cover her over. I could not stand beneath that tall, white bird and do it. I could not cover the white dress at my feet. Who is it who makes us bury ourselves this way?

I climbed out of the mouth and started up through the field. When I got to the trail on the ridge that led to the North, where later Sarah fell, from there I looked back and saw her standing in the mouth burying herself with her own clawlike hands, pulling the earth into the hole around the baby at her feet, the earth falling on the baby, Sarah lifting her feet one at a time to stand on the earth, feeding earth into the mouth while I stood high on the trail that led to the North, where later Sarah fell, she pulling in the earth while I at the lip of the cliff heard my baby crying, and I called out in a scream loud enough to awaken the beasts even in the deep caves: "No, don't, no, she is not dead."

Calling.

Leaping outward, falling, falling, my arms outstretched as a bird soaring from the high cliff in flight.

The white bird covering her over with earth.

Falling to save her, toward the earth.

For she is alive.

The air strangling me with breathlessness—

He awoke. He lay on the road trembling. The fire was burning low; it was only embers.

He pushed himself to his feet and stood, unhappy, trembling, trying to remember where he was and what he was doing here, to recall all of it, with Sarah and his child somehow part of it. How many times had he fallen from that cliff since Sarah fell? How many hundred times?

I dream such terrible dreams, he thought. Why am I afflicted in this way? Sarah, I need you.

He heard moaning, all sorrowful sounds that only a woman makes.

"Sarah, hush," he said. Then he remembered. "Ah, be quiet," he said. "Hush," he said, approaching the cart.

She is my baby, he thought, I need you, my baby grown up, with my baby's selfish instincts, with her hungry belly and her diarrhea and her quick expressions and ever-present chance of disappointment.

How sad she moans.

I need you, Sarah.

I can't stand to hear her moan.

A child is all she is. Raw instincts bundled together, responsive to any touch of affection.

"Anna, hush," he said.

Why do I care if she moans? he thought. Let her cry now, for tomorrow she cannot make any sound at all. "Cry in gushes of tears."

When I could no longer comfort Sarah, did I want her to die?

"No, no," he said, taking his child in his arms, his yielding wife before his child died, himself whom he loved no better than he loved himself, "hush, don't cry." He stroked her young body. "I'll take care of you," he said, stroking her, seeking her face with his face.

And she responded to him, moved her body in his arms and like an animal sunk her teeth deep into his shoulder, pushed him away savagely.

He fell to the road, dazed by the attack, by the fury and abruptness of it. Above him, looking down from the hooped opening of the cart, was the angry, defiant face of the girl.

7 HE AND THE GIRL were up by dawn, and he moved the bags of goods into place in the cart before he even took time to make a pot of coffee. While the coffee boiled he put the boar and the cow on their ropes. He said nothing to the girl, until finally his anger overcame him. "Look at that shirt," he said, showing her the tear, with part of his left shoulder exposed. "Look at that wound," he demanded of her.

"I never did anything—" she began, wretchedly embarrassed. "You come on me of a sleep," she said.

"Who'd you think it was, that lord of yours?"

"What would you do if a man grabs you?" she demanded of him. "A girl has to do like that."

He turned his back on her while he drank his coffee. He told her to get into the cart and hide, and only when he was through with the cup did he take any coffee to her. "We better go soon," he said, and he managed to get a rock under the hot coffee pot, so he could carry it, and he was partway to the cart with it when around the northern bend of the road appeared Sims Fisher, a tall, slender farmer from August's own community, who approached August's camp, as he approached the world in general, curiously, critically, coming along partway bent over as if moving into a wind, blinking, trying to focus on August, to decide who he might be.

"My Lord help us," August whispered fearfully, his palms damp all in a moment. He noticed that a goose stepped up on the girl's back and perched there, as if from forethought. "Sarah, help me," he murmured.

Fisher gasped on recognizing August—a forced sign of pleasure. "Here I am without a friend, with my sons trailing slow with my cattle, and I come upon a known leader in my own community," he said, beaming.

August still held the coffee pot on the rock.

"I been wanting coffee all morning and not had any, and I smell coffee here, don't I?"

"I've a fresh little bit left," August said, offering him the pot.

It didn't burn him. His hands must have been as calloused as a smith's. So were his lips apparently, for he drank directly from the pot, smacking his toothless mouth in draughts of satisfaction. "Oh my, how glad I am to meet you," he said.

"Is the road clear up ahead?" August asked him.

Fisher drank more coffee, grounds and all. "How are you, August? Tell me."

"Anxious to be home. How's the road?"

"And you living up there alone, too. You know, it's not recommended for a person to live alone, lest the spirits of the mind deceive him."

"Is that so?"

"What do you do by yourself, to distract your thoughts from your own commonness? A man's mind is a dangerous instrument, and the devil a powerful adversary."

"I think and work and read the Bible."

"August, what happened to your shoulder?"

"A limb scraped it," August said hesitantly.

"Looks like you got a deep bite there. It's bleeding still."

"I fell," August said, pulling his torn shirt over the bite. "Tell you, I'd better be under way."

"My Lord, mister. Now you tell me the truth, August. How did you get such a wound as that?"

"If you're done with my pot—" August said firmly.

"The Wright daughter, Ama, told me she was waiting at home for you," Fisher said, suddenly grinning at August, then winking at him. "She's twenty-seven, you know, ready to—"

"I'd not like to discuss any woman, much less on the road—"

"I asked her if she was missing you, and she said, 'Yes, partly.' " He laughed, winking again. "She said for you to come on home and marry her."

"I don't believe it," August said, severely annoyed.

"Why don't you marry her, August? She obviously dotes on you."

"Soon as I get my springhouse door finished and a shed for this new cow, I'll make my—I—I'm not about to discuss this with you—"

"You will put off marrying because of such trifles as that?"

"I have to make two doors. That's no trifle, is it?"

"You must not care for her a hairsbreadth if you—"

"You mind your own affairs, Fisher."

The bluntness hurt his feelings. He blinked as if he had been struck. "Oh my, on my soul," he murmured.

"I want my place properly ready for any woman I bring there," August said. "I'm doing my place well as I can; you know that."

"August, you have done it as well as anybody can," he said.

"I wouldn't want a woman to think I was marrying her so she could help build a shed or to plant or harvest for me."

"Why not?" he said.

"It's not my way, that's all. Sarah often said my sole interest in her was in the work she did—"

"But you're alone up there and that's unnatural, August. It's bound to prey on you."

"Well, I'll be going on up the road," he said abruptly.

But Fisher's eldest son came into view just then, at the head of the herd of about a dozen steers.

"There's one of my sons," Fisher said, speaking with much pride, as if his sons were royalty.

They were three straggly, unkempt, smelly fellows, as August knew them, with blond shocks of stiff hair which they rarely cut or brushed. August pulled on his jacket.

"I got fourteen head of cattle this fall, August," Fisher said. "Had twelve others to sell last spring. So what does that total?"

"I have no idea," August said.

"More'n twenty, ain't it?"

"Here," he said, trying to take the pot from his hands. "I'll be going now, Fisher."

"August, did you have a girl here last night with you?" Fisher said.

August stopped still, coldness gripping him. He saw that Fisher was studying the ground around about, the footprints and other signs.

"You had a woman here last night, I allow," Fisher said.

"How's that?" August said, helplessly confused. Her tracks were clear enough, that was true. Even he could see that.

"Small feet," Fisher said. "Injured feet." He waved his cattle back in order to protect his precious store of evidence. He called to his sons, "There's woman tracks where August spent the night."

The eldest son used a staff to help block his steers' way. The herd ganged near the cart, nervously turning. "And you always so proper, August," the son said, a big grin on his face.

"She's probably nigh," the father said, looking around with his rheumy eyes. "See her?" he asked. "Might be in them bushes peeing."

Sweat was rolling down August's body. He was in a panic, awkwardly stymied by fear, unable to think clearly. The other two sons were approaching now, too. Abruptly August moved in among the cattle and flailed them, kicked at them, and they moved forward in spite of the eldest son, who began waving his hat at them. They trampled through the camp, over the campsite, even over the remains of the fire, scattering it with a noisy complaint of smoke and sputtering. August flailed them on until there was no evidence left on the road.

The baffled eldest son stood by his baffled father, staring at the cattle moving on toward the south. Fisher threw his hat down, stomped the hat into the road in a fury of frustration.

"Now, what do you see?" August said angrily.

"Wonder if that Wright daughter followed him up this high," the eldest son said, speaking speculatively. "She never once put her shoes on, if she did," he said, and he began to laugh, then Fisher laughed, too.

"August, you got ary other drop of coffee?" Fisher asked him good naturedly.

"No, I've not," August said firmly, trying to get his cow's and boar's ropes unsnarled, for the steers had scared them. "Here, you, giddup," he said to his horse, trying to ignore the other sons who had joined them.

"He had a woman here last night," Fisher told them. "We was reading her footprints until he pushed the steers over them."

"A farmer and his wife is all," August said, and started up the road.

"Is she the one that bit you, August?" Fisher said, and his sons began to laugh at that.

"Did she bite him, papa?" one said.

"Somebody did," the old man said. "Maybe Ama did it."

August moved on, praying to get around that curve and be free of these intolerable curious neighbors—

"Hey, August, come get your pot," the old man called.

He did not. He would not go back. Let the pot be

taken. He could not face them. And she, Annalees, was huddled up in a ball as small as she could manage, on the bouncy floor of the cart, scared to death, as he could tell by peeking in at her.

And it was only just now dawn.

"I am not made for adventures," he told her, as they went along. She could hear him well enough if he walked close beside the cart. "I tell you, I always liked my own bed and to have my own room. Even as a boy when there were five of us growing up at one time, I would rather sleep on the floor than sleep with anybody else. It's not the best for my stomach to be excited first thing of a morning, either."

She said nothing. She was too scared to speak, he imagined.

"I don't intend to spend this whole day in any such agony," he said.

He passed two or three families also on their way home, who had not as yet got started this morning.

"Have they catched them?" one man called to him.

"You lost something?" he called back, though he knew full well what was meant.

"Them there runaways," the old man said.

"Where are they?" August said.

The man slapped his hip, as if slapping a horse. "I want the girl for myself, I tell ye," he said. "Have ye seen it?"

"Seen what?"

"That there mount. Two men just came by, passing the word."

At half the camps August came to, somebody asked about the runaways.

He passed several farms. Their fields were rough and splotched with stumps, even now after years of girdling and burning and sawing and sprout-cutting. Fences had been put up, usually made out of tree branches and saplings, sometimes made out of laurel and rhododendron stalks. The fences were in all cases irregular, twisty and intertwined, occasionally half-burned. The fields were scraggly with cornstalks not yet foddered, and there were patches where cabbages and other vegetables had been left to rot. In the cabin yards some of the vegetable patches had been paled with brush, to keep rabbits and chickens and other marauders out. The cabins alongside the road were one-room log structures; the doors and windows, poorly made, seemed tiny and dwarfed and the roofs appeared to be resting on walls which might topple of their own bulkiness. The roofs were of wood shingles, oak or chestnut, the latter being the more durable and the one least likely to cup.

He pulled to the side of the road to allow a flock of sheep to pass, a pretty sight in the early-morning light. A flock of sheep helped settle the worries of the mind; they were Old Testament, out of the Book itself, and were gentle and pretty. There was no fierceness to them, no crime to them.

He passed two families who had stopped to wait for a while, to make the trip take longer; they were families with children along, and for the children this was the chief outing of the year. It was even more of a holiday than Christmas, and they were excited by every jot and tittle of it, even by August's appearance with his shambly cart and boar and cow, and patient, white mare. The loose wheel squeaked, and the cart itself, having been made loose at its joints in order longer to survive the rough roads of this country, chattered in a friendly voice all its own. The geese, of course, also had to welcome or object to most everything. All in all, August supposed he did resemble to the younger people a clown with a pig following along on a rope. He waved them away, but getting rid of children is something like getting rid of beggar's lice, you have to do it one at a time. And when they came running to greet him in droves, he had more than he could handle. They overran him and threatened to overrun his cart, which set him against a bleak set of fears, indeed. So he shouted at them angrily, much to their surprise, and he even cut a staff, a tough-looking, long one, and threatened them with it, like a mad disciple.

One father, annoyed by his aggressiveness, said to him, "My girls has been around boars before, and such carts."

"That boar might rip into them," August said.

"Then it'll teach them something," the father said, so upset with him that a stupid argument would suit him as well as any other.

"Keep away, damn it," August said to the children, even in the face of parental rage.

But at one lonely stretch of road, when he was least on guard, two little boys, about eight or nine years old, dropped from the low limb of a tree, one which overhung the road, bounced off the canvas top of the cart, rolled off of it laughing, their laughter stopping in a startled gasp in the fleeting moment when they fell past the hooped, rear opening itself. All this was under an old shagbark hickory, and on the right, to the east, loomed a massive ridge a thousand feet above them; August could recall the place for a long while, so startled and scared was he. He could see himself and the two boys and the stalled cart and the attentive cow, all were marked on his mind. Fifty feet away their father huddled by his morning fire, making coffee and talking to his wife, rubbing his hands before the flames, paying no attention—a farmer named Silver from near Burnsville. The boys stood stone still, staring at the cart, their little mouths open.

August took his money from his pocket and offered each boy a dollar.

They said not a word, nor did they accept the money.

Quickly he put the two dollars on the ground and busied himself with his horse's harness. When he turned, the money was still there. A dollar was a fortune for a boy, mind you, and these two boys were standing there, watching him critically, obviously refusing the bribe.

"I have very little more to offer," he said.

"No need, mister," one of them said, his voice dry and hoarse.

The other boy said, "But you better not let mama see her."

Sturdy they were, sturdy like trees planted in rocky soil. Boys who live to themselves, on their own farm. Boys not to be bought, not by dollars anyway, not by riding horses, either, apparently, not by the fame of catching the runaway, not even that.

"She's not hungry, is she?" one asked, taking a half-chewed apple from his pocket and offering it to August.

"I think she would like that," he said, accepting it.

The other boy picked up the money and handed it to August. "I ate my apple," he said.

"This one'll do," August said. "She's eaten already once this morning."

"They're looking for her everywheres. You best take care," the older boy said.

"I will, I will." They were her friends, as August saw, and so, no doubt, were many of these other people, if he only knew which ones they were.

August had to stop to allow a flock of sheep to go by, and two women out of kindness stopped him to say they knew him, had seen him the year before on the road, and to ask how his wife was. "I recall her fondly, tall, thin lady, stiff when she walked," one lady told him, holding to his sleeve to keep him from walking on.

"In her last drive, the one two years ago, she was stiff that way," he said. "She never could accept her baby being dead, that's why."

"My Aunt Lucy never could accept a death-loss, either, until she took the baby's clothes and burned all except the bonnet, and she put that under her bed with the Bible laid on it, and she never even dreamed of that baby again. I know it sounds strange."

"Well," he said, "we didn't try that."

"What you buy in the store this year?" she asked. "Let me see."

"No cloth, no glass," he said, laughing, pulling free, flicking a switch at the horse. "I had no woman advising me this year," he said, moving on.

He heard her say to somebody, "He's the one whose woman jumped to her death."

Jumped. Jumped. Did Annalees hear her say that? Jumped. Why did that woman say jumped so plainly? How many people thought that? Oh, my God, how cruel a woman's tongue can be. Had the girl heard her? Jumped?

"How much did you pay for that there boar?" a man asked him.

"More than I should have," he said, and went on, trying to avoid conversation, risking rudeness.

"You want to trade your cow?" a man asked him.

"No, no."

"Next year I'll buy her calf."

"No, no."

"You've got a squeaky wheel on that left side," a man told him, as if the cart did not announce its ailment to the world.

He waved and went on.

"Come and sit with me," an old man said.

One invitation to conversation after another, from men and women eager to engage in talk with strangers, who wanted to exercise their roadside October privilege of meeting new people, finding out about other valleys, other ideas. "I mulched," one man, sitting beside the road, told him. That was the way he announced himself. "I mulched my corn," he said. That was his introduction of himself and his invitation to come join him, to sit with him, so he could tell about it. "With hay," he called, when August went on by.

Dogs challenged him now and then, barked at him and at the cart, where he suspected some of them could tell a human being was hiding. One big black dog

111

growled fiercely at the cart, leaped against it, scaring the cow, scaring all of them, for that matter.

"I never have knowed Caesar to be so interested in geese before," his master confessed to August, somewhat worriedly.

During the morning four separate droves of pigs were driven past them. August thanked the good Lord that drovers were, as a type, rarely anxious to converse or to mingle. Gray dust from the road, that was all there was to be seen of them; they were as dusty as their pigs and coughed a great deal. They carried staves but rarely had to use them, for the road led on within its own right, was a natural trough bordered by forests, and once put into the trough the pigs followed each other, the drovers followed along, the drovers' vision limited by the dust and the tail-ends of the pigs walking before them or, if they led the drove, limited by the vision of their own stature as leaders of pigs. In either case, they avoided conversation. The monotony of the road closed them in, along with their stock.

In midmorning August heard a raggedy hunter say Olaf was close behind, so he drove down a little trail that left the main road in order to avoid any possible meeting with him; he drove down it to the east for fifty yards or so, sat on a fallen log and fell to complaining. "How did I get into this?" he said.

The girl crawled out of the cart, hobbled on stiff legs over to one side and puked on the ground.

"It's not for human beings, such anxiousness as this," he said.

"Those there geese smell," she said.

"Well, I know," he said. "Look here, you better stay hid, or you'll be seen."

She crawled off behind a stand of bushes and he heard her groaning. He supposed her bowels and stomach were still upset.

"My hands have got a tremble most of the time," he said.

She secluded herself until he got up to go, then without a word she appeared and climbed back into the cart.

Sometimes she dared to look out the front of the cart, watching the road ahead, leaf-colored and sunny at certain places. If the road had nobody in sight, and if they could see along a big sweep, perhaps along a mountain's wall, she would look out.

"I gave you the best food you ever ate," he told her. "Then you took to my arm, took to cannibalism."

"You come on me unawares," she said contentiously. "I never was so surprised . . ."

"I ought to make you hold out your arm for me to take a bite of," he said.

"I've fought off men afore, you can believe."

"You thought I was Olaf?" he asked.

"I fought off Sims for all one morning."

"That boy who helped you escape, then left you?" he said. "You thought I was him?"

"Sims got lost is all," she said. "We got parted, and I didn't dare call for him."

"He was accustomed to grabbing hold of you, was he?"

"He tried to," she said.

"He your man?" he asked jealously.

113

"I don't welcome everybody who comes by, I'll say that for myself—"

"Like Olaf?" he said.

She said nothing. Apparently she wasn't going to talk about that.

"I ought to take my bite out of you wherever I please," he said. "I can put brandy on a rag and try to wipe a place clean, and I can take a big bite." His voice had taken on a tinge of bitterness which surprised him. He was angry with her for biting him, that was true, and he was jealous of her, but he was amused by last night's incident, too. "Is Olaf your father?" he asked her.

"Why, I 'spect he is," she said briefly, and withdrew into the cart.

She asked once if he had a witch's bone with him, and he thought she said a wishbone. "No, I haven't," he said.

"My mama has two, but she wouldn't let me have one of them."

"Why not, if she has two?" he said.

"She was 'fraid I would kill somebody with it."

He had no idea what she meant. "Kill somebody with a wishbone?" he said.

"A witch's bone," she said. "You know."

When he admitted he did not know, she hesitated to tell him anything more, and it took many questions before he found out that a witch's bone was useful in casting spells on one's enemies, even to death, and to ward off spells cast by others. He asked her how such an instrument could be obtained.

"From a cat," she said.

"What color cat?"

"Black."

"Male or female?"

"Male."

"What age?"

She giggled. "Why, you know."

"And what do I do with the cat?"

"Drop it into boilin' water," she said.

"Dead?" he said.

"Live," she said. There she sat—rather, there she crouched at the front of the cart, looking out at the road, calmly glancing from time to time at him, as contented as if she were explaining to him how to make biscuits. "And when it has boiled until its bones come free of its flesh, you take the pot to the river and throw the broth and the flesh and bones in, and one bone will always come to the surface and will float upstream."

A chill came over him, but at the same time he had an impulse to laugh, for it was so utterly incredulous. He ventured to ask her if she had ever known a witch.

"Four," she said at once.

"Was your mother one of them?"

"No," she said, laughing.

"Can a man be a witch?"

"A man can be a conjurer, but he can't teach another man to be one, and I think a man can't be a witch. And a black person can't conjure a white person."

"No, I imagine not."

"I never have done it," she said.

"No, of course not, but how is it done?" he said.

"I don't want to be one," she said.

"But I wonder how it is done."

That was all she would say about it.

August had no timepiece. As a boy, that was what most in life he wanted. His father had a silver English watch and wanted a silver chain to go with it. As August looked back and thought about it, his father saved the money for that chain many times, and each time he spent the savings for some other need. To his death he used a leather fob.

August's ambition as a boy was to have a watch and maybe a chain. What if Olaf as a reward had offered a watch and chain, he asked himself, would that have attracted you more than a Virginia horse? Is it that you don't need a riding horse?

He was not conscious of danger that afternoon, not in the least, which surprised him. He knew he was in danger, but he suffered no effect of it. He was astonished at himself, to find himself walking free and in the clear, walking along this road, August C. King—whatever your name is, whoever you are—walking on this road without fear, transporting her, the object of a far-ranging search. August, I scarcely know you in your greatness, he told himself. And, indeed, he was a new character, a stranger, as in a play, not himself at all.

Is it not true that God marks us, chooses us, puts his finger on our forehead, says, "You," conjures us, just as it is true that lightning will strike a tree—not any special tree, not a tree necessarily that stands the highest or is the largest or is the oldest in the field. Lightning makes its own secret selection.

Lightning is striking you, August, he said to himself. And he felt proud of it. He felt secure because of it, too.

He was honored by the distinction. From the height of this distinction he could look back on himself of yesterday, on that common man weighted down with a load of ordinary cares.

Yet she was not as calm. She was jittery. She was sick. Of course, it was true that she was in even a more precarious position than he, because she didn't know as yet to trust him. Even he was a danger to her, as was everybody else.

"I'm not free myself," he said, walking along, the idea coming to him all of a sudden. "If I'm not free, how can you be free?" He had not been free yesterday and was not free today; he was bound yesterday and today by sets of outrageous circumstances that had trapped him. When was a man free ever? The shape of our face, the health of our hand, all the more important matters tend to be decided for us, by birth or accident or God or Fate or chance or accident or whatever, or by our parents, our brothers, our sisters, our friends, our lovers, our haters in the day, our haters in the night, our beasts, our brutes, our paths on the hills, our oak tree felled by lightning.

A hog drove went past. When it was gone, Annalees stuck her head outside to ask if she could have something to eat. "It's after noon," she said, looking up through the leaves, trying to see the sun.

"I made a sun clock on my floor at home," he told her proudly, pleased to be reminded of it. "Cut it into the boards."

"On your floor?" she said. She had a delightful way of expressing astonishment.

"Using the window and a stick."

"I never heard of such a clock."

"I haven't either," he said.

"What your wife say?"

"She tolerated it."

"Law, I'd like to have a floor clocked."

"It didn't work on cloudy days, of course, or at night. It didn't work well any time, to be honest about it."

"Can you make one out of doors?"

"I don't know. We can try it, once we get home," he said.

Strange, strange to hear himself say that. Days, weeks, months would be needed to develop such a sun system. Did he mean for her to stay with him? Was he putting Annalees in the house he owned? He had not even disturbed Sarah's things, her collection of medicines, her clothes, her linen, her necklace of bright stones, her glass-jeweled comb, her dish or glass.

Annalees seemed to have placed no importance on what he had said. "I saw a man in Morganton cut his cornbread with a knife," she told him solemnly. "I never saw anybody do it that way."

"How does Olaf cut his cornbread?" he asked.

"Same as you."

"Well, how do I do it?" he said. "I don't recall noticing."

"Law, don't you know?"

"I suppose I would cut it or break it as I pleased," he said.

"Nobody cuts his bread," she said emphatically.

Soon thereafter, a man named Silas Turner, sitting dejectedly beside the road, sadly watched them approach. "They catched her, so I'm out a horse," he told August.

"Oh, that's too bad," August said. "Where did they catch her?"

"Catched her up ahead some'ers," he said.

"Well, I was certain they would," August said.

On down the road four men were discussing having seen the male runaway. Several boys were even now beating the bushes with sticks, trying to flush him into the open again. "I saw him running," a man said, "then he fell, and when I got to the place, he was gone as sure as if'n he's a ghost."

"A devil, more'n likely," another man said to him.

"Black devil," another man said.

"I saw him over there," an old man said, pointing toward a spot in the woods off to the west side of the road. "I think it was him I saw," he said. "They caught the girl near here, so he's bound to be about."

A planter had parked his four big wagons and his big horses and oxen along one side of the road, and he was in the east woods calling to two black men who were beating the rhododendron bushes. "More to the left," he said. "I tell you, he went in there." Suddenly he moved to a wagon and got his rifle, aimed it quickly and fired into the bushes, fired near where one of his own black men stood. That poor scared man fell to the ground and lay there groveling. "Go on in where I shot at," the planter shouted at him. The black man, trembling, got to his feet.

August rode on by, the planter paying little attention to him.

At a narrow, rutted place, one used for passing, he pulled off the road, and Annalees crept into the woods to relieve herself. He could hear her moaning. He waited, trying to calm his nerves, which had grown more and more inflamed since that gun was fired.

"We got a sorry meal to eat," he called to Annalees. He had the loaf of cornbread, that was all. "I'm going to cut this bread with a knife," he told her.

She giggled. He heard that quite clearly, so she was not far away, and she was not distressed, not in any way defeated.

He broke the bread into two pieces, then remembered his jug of brandy and got that out. He stood waiting for her, entertaining himself with self-assurances. He was standing there alone when a horseman came around the northern bend, moving wearily, slowly, but when he saw August he raised his hand in a salute and came riding forward with a flurry of noise and dust.

"Ah, there you are," he said. It was Olaf Singleterry. "I must have ridden past you earlier on."

"I'm told you caught your girl," August said, trying to appear casual.

"Who told you that?" he said. "The boy's been sighted a time or two, but not her."

"Men on the road tell me she's found."

"It's not so," he said. "You know where she is, do you?"

"No, no," August said.

"That fellow, that tall, lanky farmer, the first one on

the road at my camp this morning, that fellow who looks into every pot—"

"I know him," August said.

"He told me you camped near me last night."

"Don't you know that? Don't you remember my leaving your fire after dark to make my own camp?"

Olaf considered that, then shook his head. "Don't recall," he said. He seemed to be worried about his lapse of mind. "Well, sir," he said, more alert suddenly, "my girl might have been at your camp. Yesterday two hunters from nigh home trailed her all day long, said she left a trail as easy to follow as a reel-footed bear; even left torn pieces of her dress, left blood marks from her feet. When dark came they were not more than two hundred yards from my camp but never knew it, still on the girl's trail."

"She was trying to find you, Olaf," August said.

"She never came into my camp. This morning the hunters said she skirted my camp and went on another five, ten minutes of limping, then ventured onto the road itself, where her tracks have all been trampled out. She must have come near your camp," he said.

"Yes," August said, trying to act unconcerned, "but I never camped till well after sundown, did I?"

"Even so," Olaf said cautiously.

"You think maybe she came to steal something from me?"

Olaf shook his head irritably. "No, no," he said, and dismounted abruptly, stared at August for a moment before with a grunt he strode to the cart, where roughly, before August could even try to stop him, he threw a coat to one side and shoved the coffee sack out

121

of the way. He stood staring at the bags of flour, sugar, salt, all innocent possessions. For a minute or two he stood there. "Ah, I would have sworn—" he murmured. "Ahhhhhh." He cursed quietly for a while, an accompaniment to his disappointment. He still stood with his back to August, looking at the pile of supplies. When he turned wearily he said, "I did so hope to find her." He shook his head in bafflement, like a stymied bull. "That farmer, whatever his name was, said there were footprints . . ." His voice trailed off.

"If she came to my camp, would she have been hungry?" August asked. "I'm wondering why she would come to my camp at all."

"Well, she might have been hungry, poor thing."

"What would she steal? What do they eat, anyway?"

"What do they eat?" he said. "What do you mean?"

"Milk?" August said. "Do they drink milk?"

"What do you think they eat? They eat anything. What does it matter? I want to find her, I tell you, and she's near here, and was near me, near you last night."

"I wondered what she might try to steal from me, that's all."

"She's not a thief, I told you," he said angrily.

"Don't shout at me, Olaf."

Olaf glared at him, stunned, for he had been surprised by a show of strength from so mild a man. He gestured helplessly finally. "I was certain it was you. I've told people up ahead it was you, though I never used your name. What is your name?"

"What did you say?"

"I said she's with a man with a cart and a young Jersey cow tied to it, for that's what that farmer said. I forgot his name. What is your name?"

"I don't appreciate your using me—"

"If they stop you, tell them she's not with you, that's all."

"Stop me?" August said.

"I knew you had her, once that farmer told me a girl's footprints were at your camp—"

"A farmer and his wife," August said. "I tried to explain—"

"And where are they?" Olaf said.

"They went on ahead."

"Why didn't you travel with them?"

"We argued, that's all."

"About what?"

"Infant baptism."

Olaf stood before him, frowning at him. At last he shrugged helplessly, and a strong sense of power came to August, richer than any he had previously in his life known, for here he was, challenging one of the region's richest, most powerful men, and he was defeating him. He even had enough capacity to feel sorry for him. "What you think of my new cow, Olaf?" he said.

Olaf blinked and coughed from surprise. He turned away and spat on the road, then wiped a fat hand over his face. "Some nigras are worth more than wealth," he murmured. "You get fond of one now and then."

"I'll go ahead now, before your wagons get here, Olaf," August said.

"They're ahead of you," he said. "How did I pass you? Did you leave the road?"

"I did, yes," August said.

Olaf mounted. For a while he frowned down at August, studying him. "It's all too murky to be seen through."

"No trouble," August said.

When Olaf had gone around the curve in the road, August took his cow into the woods and tied her to a tree. Annalees came through the woods and crouched nearby. She was subdued and humble, was murmuring to herself, maybe a prayer, maybe a plea to some ghosts or lord. "What did he say about me?" she said.

With his knife he killed his young cow.

Not with any emotion, either. The red blood on the green vines and the galax, bright red, and yet no worry. He was the Jew in the temple slaying the brought sacrifice; no thought was given to it. One did what was his duty.

The raspy noise in the throat of the cow.

Why had he not flailed it and sent it running through the woods; it would seek to find its way home, surely.

Why did I kill it? he wondered.

Was there something bloody in him, as there was blood on his hands. As on his Jesus. "God knows, we are such mysteries," he said aloud.

"I never saw anybody kill a milch cow before," Anna said, her girl's face poutingly drawn into old-face wrinkles, her eyes squinting at the bleeding, gasping body on the green bed before her.

"I haven't either," August said.

"Why did you do it?"

"Why?" he demanded of her, as if her question made no sense to him. "Why do you ask me?" he said, baffled by his own confusion and irritated with her. It was so much easier if he could do what he felt he must do, and not be asked why he did it.

124

8 "YES, I SAW two hunters in the woods," Annalees told him as they rode on, she in the cart. "They
walked like statues, two of them. I saw them twice
yesterday. I never felt more scared."

"Young men?" he said. "Long hair, tied behind?"

"Yes."

"Leather pants and jackets? Frills on their jackets?"

"Yes."

"I saw them last at the Inn," he said.

They were approaching Buffer, which was a scattered settlement, and beyond it was a big field that
nature had cleared. Annalees was sitting up in the cart,
talking to August, her voice trembling, even though she
whispered.

"They trailed me all yesterday," she said. "You heard
what he said."

"Well, I know," he said. "I'm not a match for them,
either."

"Aren't you?" she said.

He was surprised to hear her ask that. Could it be she
thought he was? Maybe, since he had stood his ground

with Olaf, she thought he could stand his ground with anyone, for Olaf was the great lord of all men, wasn't he? "I wonder if they're trailing us now, or if they're up in front of us," he said.

"Would they go home?" she said.

"No home, no home," he said. "They never will give up a hunt, from what I know of them. And the longer and harder it is, the better."

Along the way a poor man, dressed in rags, called to August, asked if he had food to give him.

"I think not," August said. "But the two slaves were seen back that a way."

The man swung around and started running, fast as he could go.

Just ahead August came upon a man leading six goats to market, and the herder said, "The buck nigger was caught trying to skirt the Buffer field."

"That so?" August said, moving on toward it. "They didn't catch Sims," he later told Annalees. "It's another rumor. The rumors blow here like leaves in a storm."

Along the approach to the field many families had run their wagons into the woods and were making camp, planning to wait here until next day. Always many such families were here, for the Buffer field was the best place along the northern road to trade, to get rid of balky stock or bulky goods, to hire drovers, to buy wheels or rent oxen. Just this side of the field, which extended up to the ball of the hill, a bold stream of water came into a bigger stream, so one could safely drink the water from the little stream and not worry about excrement and garbage being dumped into the bigger one.

August's cart was approaching the joining of the streams, where two privies were built over the water. He saw he was going to have to wait to cross the ford, for just now two drovers were trying to drive their pigs across, so he stopped back a ways on the road and pretended to be greasing his left wheel. One of the drovers' pigs got carried off in the stream, and two drovers ran along the bank, shouting encouragement and instructions to it, then one splashed into the river and finally got his pig, carried it in his arms back to shore, the pig squealing in terror, men laughing goodnaturedly.

Beyond the river, in the field, other men had games going, among them a racing game with several horses involved. Higher on the hill August could see that a caber tossing was taking place.

At the top of the field two big locust poles had been set firmly in the ground, one on each side of a raised platform, a third post secured to their tops; this was the main butchering place for hogs and cattle. Most always fresh meat could be purchased or traded for there. A crowd of men, perhaps fifty or sixty of them, had gathered at the poles just now for what appeared to be a preaching, and others were going up that way.

"I'm going to have to put my boar in the wagon with you," August told Annalees.

"He'll paw me to death, if the water gets in here."

"I don't know that there will be any water get in there," he said. "You put the coffee beans and the pots on the bottom."

Down the road behind them came another wagon. Its driver acted as if he didn't see August's cart waiting, but when he started by, August called to him, said he was waiting in the shade, then he moved out in front and approached the river.

"I'll leave the boar on the rope," he told Annalees. "He can swim."

Looking across the stream he saw that a cabin had been built in the field and somebody had lettered a sign reading IN. Meaning INN, he supposed. Not much of an IN or an INN, the best he could tell from here.

"There," Annalees said suddenly, gasping.

He saw them, too, in that instant saw the two lean hunters from Hobbs unbend from their crouch, rise to their feet, their eyes glinting like stones. They had been waiting at the ford, no doubt studying each wagon or cart or rider who came along, surveying all that passed. My Lord in Heaven, there was no way on earth to sneak past them, August realized, and there was no way to turn from them now.

He climbed into the cart, crouched at the very front of it, as was usual for him at a fording. "I don't know how this will do," he said.

The road here took a deep dip as it fell off toward the water. The stream was about fifty feet across and was particularly rowdy just now, rolling and pitching over the rocks. "How you?" August called to the two hunters.

On the other side of the river a group of drovers waited to cross, watching. The two hunters came forward to stop August.

"They saw the nigger girl back up the way," August said to them, pointing up the hill behind him.

The hunters came on. "How's that?" one said.

August lashed his horse. "Nigger girl," he said to them, "men are running her through laurel now."

"Where?" one of the hunters said.

"There you go," he said, pointing up the hill, "that crest up there. A man had her, man with a cart with a Jersey cow tied to it."

The statement must have overcome their doubts, for they turned and started running up the road, just as August's cart, groaning, rumbling, hit the water of the fording place, jolting into the water. His geese objected hoarsely, his boar began the most awful squealing. Annalees found herself pinned under bags of sugar and flour as the cart splashed through the water, dangerously rocking and pitching.

"Hold on," several drovers shouted, laughing.

The boar tore free and went washing downstream, squealing in such terror that most everybody nearby turned to watch him, and the drovers started yelling at August, as if he didn't know his boar was in the water. There the boar went, floating off toward Tennessee, making the most urgent cries, but August couldn't stop, couldn't leave the girl. He closed his mind, even lashed his horse yet another time, and his cart, groaning, came up out of the water, gushing water from its wheels, the squeal of the pig filling his mind.

One of the drovers shouted at him, "Why you let your boar go like that?" He was furious about it, apparently.

"No need," August said, "he's lame."

"Lord 'a mercy, fellow," the drover said, "even if he's lame he needn't drown."

Way off downriver August could hear the boar squealing, a pitiful wail which jarred his nerves, for he had liked him dearly and he needed him at home. Many people were looking at him strangely now, no doubt wondering what sort of callous fool he was, what in the world had come over him.

"We got over all right," he told Annalees, his voice trembling like a schoolboy's.

She was crying. She was huddled on the floorboards of the cart whispering to her ghostly saints, frightened to incoherence.

One man, a Thompson, recognized August. "How you, August?" he said.

"I'm all right," August said, switching his horse, moving on steadily up the hill.

"They got the boy up there at the posts," Thompson said, gesturing toward the top of the hill.

"All right," August said, waving to him as he went on, trying to stay free of him.

In view close by were perhaps twenty fires, where people were talking and trading and fussing at their children. There were horses and pigs and cattle and chickens everywhere. There were forty or fifty wagons parked in a massive disarray. There was even a coon on a string, a small, bright-faced boy leading it along. Oxen stood with lowered heads and glowered at him.

"What he mean?" Annalees said from the cart. "Is Sims up there?"

"No, no. They've caught a boy who owes me three dollars," August said. "Last year he borrowed from a dozen of us, coasting on his father's name."

They were passing near a pen where a promoter had unleashed a dog and a groundhog to fight; he wanted a penny from anybody who wanted to watch, and fifty or sixty men and boys were trying to find places to see the fight whether they all had paid a penny or not; they were standing on wagons and rocks and on each other's shoulders. From the cart, as he rolled past, August saw the dog lunge at the groundhog, but the groundhog at once got the dog's leg in his mouth and broke it. He broke it in one chomp. The dog let out a bellow of pain, then sank his teeth into the groundhog's neck, so there they rolled, the men shouting out encouragement to one or the other, closing in around the pen as August rolled on, the men in a fever because of the pain and blood and fierceness.

August heard two people as they walked up toward the top of the field talking about having got him, having got the buck at last, but Annalees couldn't have heard them with her ear pressed against the floorboards. Even then he saw, far up on the hillside at the butchers' poles, a black on the platform. People were gathering around him, no doubt were interrogating him, scaring him, trying to find out where the girl was. God knows, August knew he couldn't go that way. He turned off the road and crossed a patch of grass to a maple tree, getting the cart off to as private a place as he could, telling Annalees his wheel needed care. "You stay in there. Don't even look out," he said, afraid she might see Sims being persecuted, for Sims was only two hundred feet or so away from them, in clear view.

August sat down on the ground, weakened by the confusion in his own mind.

"All right, all right," he told the horse, for she was scared. "I know," he said. "It was a wild crossing of a river, I admit. And we're in a fix now."

No telling what in God's world those white men, what Olaf, would do to Sims, August thought.

Annalees said to him from the cart, "Where are those two leathered men?"

"Back up the other way," he said. "They're hunting for you in the wrong direction just now."

"Will they come after us here?"

"I don't think so," he said. She's worried more about them than about Sims, he realized. Does she know about Sims? he wondered.

"I never knew it'd be like this to get to the North," she said.

He smiled at that, wondering about it, whether she had meant for it to amuse him. "The Hebrews took forty years to get to the Promised Land," he told her.

"They never rode in carts forty years," she said, "with three geese and a hundredweight of flour."

Men and women were trudging up the road toward the black man on the platform, but only one man said anything to August; he asked why hadn't August tried to save his boar.

"He was lame anyway," August told him.

How many lies have you told on this journey, August? he asked himself. All last year you told no lies at all, not a one, and here on this journey you've told half a dozen. No, more than that.

"Come see it," one of the men, one of the farmers going up the road, called to him.

"In a minute," August said.

A cloudy day now, no stark sun showing, not just now. The air was moist, as if preparing for rain.

The dog and groundhog had got done fighting, so

that audience was going up to see the other show, their faces set with hard, tough grins, their teeth showing, as they steeled themselves to witness one more ordeal of pain. August left the cart, went closer to the road to see their faces, drawn by the danger.

"Beat that big dog," one man said to August. "Think of that."

"They ain't found her yet, have they?" one man said to another.

"The boy will tell where she is," a man replied, wiping his slobbery mouth with the sleeve of his coat. "Them planters will free his tongue."

"Where do they get all the dogs they fight the hogs with?" a man said.

"A planter will be fierce with his niggers, if needs be. Has to be, or they'll all run away."

"Seems like a dog would have beat a hog, if they had used a proper dog."

"Olaf took delivery of him near the river, paid over the fifty dollars, said then and there he'd have the truth or tatter him one. I expect he will, too, he was so white and furious."

August had a sudden impulse to flee. He could run across the field and reach the woods. He could hide there and look out at the field and see his cart, watch his horse, his supplies. He could huddle in safety, at least in comparable safety, there.

What if they find her? What if they find me? he thought. What was he to say to them? What in the world could he think to say to them? It is too much for the human mind to endure, for flesh and bones to live with.

"You don't think that Marshall fellow uses sick dogs, then makes money betting, do you?" a man asked his companion. "He could use sick dogs and a well ground-hog."

"Of course, if the nigger don't know where she's at, not much he can say to save himself, is there?" a man said.

Sims' life was valuable, as was the girl's, but it was not within August's powers to help both of them. Maybe the girl would willingly surrender to save Sims—that thought occurred to him, but he didn't want to lose her that way. I must save her from herself, her selflessness, he thought, I must save her from even seeing Sims being questioned. Drive through the field itself, he thought, go around the crowd, try to regain the road on the other side of them, where it re-enters the woods.

He had to move slowly, avoiding one great rock and then another, one little camp, then another, nodding to the women and children. The main crowd was above him and to his left as he walked along beside his mare.

A drunk man, stumbling, begging for pity, begging for a drink, came toward him.

"No, no, go away," August said.

The drunk held out his hand for a penny.

"I have none," August said.

The drunk followed along, so August hurriedly found the jug of brandy and gave it to him. "Drink," he said. "But not deeply. One gulp."

At that moment he saw a boy approach his horse.

"No, no," he said, and moved to stop the boy from coming any closer to the cart. The horse started on.

August ran to grab the harness to stop her. "A minute more," he said to her, the whole world twirling around him, confusion everywhere, people walking past him, past the cart, and when he turned to retrieve his jug, he saw the drunk standing at the tailgate of the cart, his hand extended, trembling violently even as he held the jug out before him to set it inside he cart, his stare fixed on the cart, on the girl, his mouth open, his red eyes blazing with frightened knowledge.

August hurried to him, pushed the jug back into his arms. "There, drink it," he said.

"Ga, ga, ga," the drunk said, and choked, began to cough, his eyes watering.

"Drink," August said, and pushed the jug deep into his arms.

The drunk put the jug to his lips and drank deeply of it.

"Drink," August said, and watched him as he drank all he could, until he gasped, then sank to the ground, to his knees, coughing, the jug still in his hands. "It's yours," August said to him, and backed away from him. "Do you hear me?" he said, his own voice echoing in his head.

The drunk, coughing, some of the brandy even now seeping down from his saggy lips, suddenly looked up at August, his red eye focused on him. "I see such sights," he said.

"Sights not so," August said, "not of this world."

"I can't touch what I see sometimes."

"No, it's not there," August said.

"I saw the girl."

"It's the liquor," August said, clicking his tongue in

135

sympathy. "Take some more." August waited, watching the drunk until he saw him once more raise the jug to his lips.

"Drown him, drown him," he prayed, hurrying to his horse, so dizzy he could scarcely remain erect.

The earth righted itself. Nobody seemed to notice him. The drunk was now a long way behind him, still sitting on the ground. Who would believe him now? August's body was hot, was in a fever, but his mind was clearer than before. He had only a little ways to go to reach home, once he got free of this field.

The crowd on the hill started singing a hymn. A big-voiced man lined it out for them. My preacher, August thought, the one who serves my church. He could see him.

"Which do you think is mentioned more often in the Bible, Annalees, cattle or goats?" August said to her, anxious to talk, to occupy his mind and hers, to shut out his fears. "I used to read the Bible day and night, after Sarah fell. I counted what animals were mentioned in it, marked them on the floor. Had a place for donkeys, fowls, cattle, sheep, goats, had them at different places on the floor."

He heard a deep voice giving orders. Was it the preacher's?

"What's that voice, do you know?" she said.

A gasp from the people.

"Some man or other," he said.

"Sounds like a pain," she said.

"It's a worship. You keep your face down, you hear me? They have a service up the hill, and I'm going around it. Let me tell you, in the Bible, if a steer was to be the sacrifice, it had to be a red male and not have any blemishes on it. I asked the German why it couldn't have blemishes and he said maybe the priest who wrote the rules got to keep the hide. That's not a holy reason, is it? I think it won't do. But in any case the priest slew the steer, then flayed it. What you suppose that means, that word 'flayed'? I asked the German and he admitted he didn't know."

"It sounds so strange," she said, "the sounds are so strange."

"Then they cut the meat up and washed the innards and the legs, sprinkled the blood on the altar and burned it all, burned his guts, all of him. It was to the glory of God they did it."

The cart bounced along. They were two thirds of the way to the woods. Suddenly a cry. A high, vibrating cry of a man. Then silence from the crowd, then a moan from the crowd. August's horse stopped. He stopped. He saw Annalees was on her knees, staring toward the crowd.

He couldn't see Olaf up there, or the Negro, Sims. The preacher, standing on the platform, was in a trance. August saw that the men had hung a steer from the locust crosspiece, as they often did. They had split the steer down the belly and backbone, as they always did. "Stay down, Anna," he said.

Slowly, as if feeling his way through a murky darkness, he moved on, the squeaky cart following.

"They never did sacrifice pigs, the Hebrews never did," he said. "Never would eat them, either. Wouldn't eat short ribs, bacon, ham, none of it. Sausage."

"Where is Sims?" she said from the cart. "Did they catch Sims?"

"Not like us," he said. "The Jews were a people same as we, but they had different ways from us."

"What's hanging up over there?"

"I killed my cow, you know it, Annalees?" he said. "I lost my boar in the river."

"What is it?" she said.

"A steer or a hog. Every time I've passed those butchers' posts there's been a hog or steer hanging there."

The crowd was moving now. Men and boys. Mostly men. Men were moving toward them, grimly smiling, held in a trance of some sort, as if terror were inside them. August climbed into the cart, crouched near her. The cart kept on moving slowly through the field. The crosspiece was over to the left, still above them on the hill, somewhat behind them now.

"What do you think is mentioned more in the Bible," he said to her, "cattle or goats?"

She moaned, a deep, retching sound of distress.

"The German guessed cattle. If it was our own people, it would be cattle. Or hogs. But the Hebrews were more interested in goats. They were a good deal more interested in goats and turtledoves than I've ever been."

A drover had tried to lead his drove of pigs southward around the crowd. The men kicked at the pigs; pigs went running all over the hillside, the men cruelly kicking them and shouting them on. One man stabbed, slashed a pig with his knife. He opened the pig's throat. See it bleed as it runs.

Men were filtering past the cart now, slapping their

138

hands on the cart, affirming their masculine prowess.

The bleeding pig walked slower and slower, moving with a red trail down the hill, moving slovenly with lowered head.

"Hush, stay quiet," August said to Annalees. He crouched in the cart, so that his body helped to hide her. He crouched over her, with the geese around her and him. She was trembling. Well, this is the road that leads to the North, he thought.

"You missed the show," one of the men said to August.

"Hey, August, what'd you do with your pretty cow?" a man called to him.

"Traded her," he called back at once.

"Where's your boar?"

"Lost him," he said.

"Lost him in the river," somebody else said. "Didn't you see that crossing while ago, before they killed that man?"

"Hush, hush," August whispered. Oh, God, be quiet, he thought, knowing all along, knowing before he heard, yes, or saw again the two halves of the brute turning just now in opposite directions so that the halves grossly formed the body of a man, then separated and became two men, one of them headless, looking off toward opposite mountains of this wild land.

He stopped the cart. He couldn't move forward any farther, couldn't think how to proceed. Let them find me out, he thought. Let them uncover my sins and hang me, too. I can't flee any farther. Let them find us both here in the field and do their worst to us. A terror comes, so dark and dense, no light shines through.

9 JUST AS THE FLESH will sometimes achieve the deadening of its pain, so the mind will achieve immunity from terror. When August awakened to consciousness he was relaxed and calm, and found himself crouched in the cart near the girl, as before, his body warmly coated with thick perspiration. He became aware of a soft-accented voice, an outlander planter's voice. "Get out of the way," the planter was saying to somebody. "Listen heah," he said, "listen heah, I got to git home tonight."

Of course, being a planter, he expected his own way, even about the road, which had its own way, as you have seen, which sets up its own tests of the beasts and men who use it. Listen, if a brute goes down this road, a colt, a calf, a shoat, consider the immense dangers, for should it get its foot the least bit wounded, its life's fate is sealed. It will be eaten, if not by a wolf or fox along the way, then by its master, or clubbed by him in his exasperation and thrown off a cliff, for he never expected all his stock to reach the destination, anyway. Consider the way of justice here on the road for the brutes and fowl, then see if there is a different law for the man dangling back there on the butchers' tree.

"Git that wagon off this heah road," the planter said, not to August but to a farmer whose big wagon had broken down.

A gang of wagons was accumulating as a consequence of the disabled wagon, there at the edge of the field where the forest road resumed like the spout of a funnel. A score of men were now walking forward to lend a hand. They were hitting the cart and saying, "Come on here," to August, and such as that.

He watched them and others try to move the wagon, a big one loaded with expensive goods. They tried to push the wagon off the road. "We'll have to unload it ever bit, I'm afeared," a man said angrily.

The farmer who owned the wagon and his wife were deeply worried, were indeed frantic by now. "Now, will you be careful of my things?" she said.

A hundred feet away the body dangled from the posts, the half-bodies turned in the shadows thrown by the light of God Almighty on this field.

Other men were sloshing their way forward, cursing the broken wagon. There was a nervousness to them, an intensity that had come from the execution. There were perhaps forty men in that jumble of arms and legs and mud, trying to unload the wagon. Other wagons and horses and stock, in trying to get past the funnel the forests formed, had bogged down and tangled.

"Come on," two men said to August, and stopped to wait for him.

He left the cart and went along, nodding agreeably to them, for he couldn't afford a confrontation of any

141

sort, no, not of any sort, and he mingled with the others, finally taking his place in a line of men who were passing on bags and boxes from the wagon, a mirror, a drawer full of women's clothes, a blanket chest, a sack of seed, all the while conscious of his cart, of Annalees being in the cart—

"He broke his wagon in the road, blocks all the traffic for a hundred yards," one farmer said, blaming the wagon for an anger of his own, one too deep for the wagon to cause or the farmer to comprehend, coursing with his blood ceremonially.

"Shouldn't bring a big, bastard wagon like this on the road," another said angrily, passing on to August a fifty-pound bag of flour, which he passed on to a man from Andrews, whose face was contorted, was stymied by some deep fury or thirst. "Slow up traffic, mire down in the mud, flounder in the crossings."

"Had to kill that nigger, didn't we, Jim?" the man from Andrews said.

The man Jim began to curse, a vile and liquid sound of oaths and obscenities, seeking to comfort himself. "Clear all the wagons and niggers off this here road," he said.

August thanked God Annalees couldn't hear them. He wondered if she would have been dismayed by their vileness or if it would be a customary sound to her—if in the slave hovels she had found obscenities to be the ordinary accompaniment to daily living. The hatred in their voices, the evil spilling from the cracks in their bodies, she would have heard before.

"Had no business running off," the man Jim said.

"This whole country be full of niggers running off," a man said.

142

"Get so we can't move on the road without niggers running off."

"Find that there girl next," the man Jim said.

"Rip her up the middle."

"Might not," Jim said. "He wants her, he says."

"For hisself," a sweaty man said, and belched. "He'll rip her hisself."

"I'll see her split, myself," Jim said.

"Set her on a pole," a man said.

"Strip her naked, let her wiggle."

"Strip her, yeh."

"Might be his own family that's run off," a man said.

August dropped a box of nails—it was heavier than he had planned for.

"Get that up, damn it," Jim said to him angrily.

"Who you talking to?" August said, glaring up at him.

"I—I wasn't meaning anybody. It's the way the day is," Jim said, confused.

"Well, hell," August said, and picked up the box and passed it on. He noticed that the last men in the line were dumping the stuff roughly on the field, were scattering it, had even broken open the chests and had torn open the bags. He saw them scatter the nails, along with everything else.

"Don't you bring ary busted wagon this here road again," a man told the hapless farmer, who was babbling, pleading.

"What Olaf'll do," Jim said, handing August a bag of coffee, "is get the girl for hisself."

"Oh, my lord, yes," the sweaty man said, handing Jim a stack of stoneware dishes.

Jim threw them to the ground. "I never had no such dishes," he said. "What the hell that man bring up here,

what he think a wilderness is, a place for white plates?
Does he think it's a white-plated place, tell me?"

"Break them," somebody said.

"Split him down the middle this evening, if we find
him," a man said.

"Who?" August said.

"Man who helps her," the man said.

"Split him and her both," a farmer said.

Oaths began again to pour out of Jim like liquid from
a jug. "I got something for her."

"Help a nigger?" a man said. "Who'd help a nigger?"

"So they say. Man with a damn Jersey cow."

"You can imagine what he's doing to her every curve
of the road," Jim said. "Pretty girl, they say."

"Better he milks his cow."

"Olaf wants her back, for himself, don't he?" a man
said.

A few of the men at the end of the line were putting
on the women's bonnets and even the dresses, laughing
at each other. A man was running about with the mirror, showing different ones their images.

"Stick a pole in her."

"That buck nigger would do it to her, you can bet
your life," a man said.

"Do it to any woman, once he runs off," Jim said.
"I've heard of niggers—"

"Stick a pole in her."

The mirror was broken now, smashed into many
pieces, and the pieces were being passed about, so the
men could see themselves. The pieces were twinkling,
winking in the sunlight.

When they find her, and it might be any time now,

they will find me, too, August thought. Walk, walk slowly to the woods, August, casually step into the woods, then God knows, flee. Flee with your cowardly face hid from view.

Is it the girl that keeps me from fleeing? he wondered. Tell me what it is. If caught, she will be treated better than me. Olaf probably won't harm her. But he will harm me. Why do I stay? Is it because of the girl's need for freedom? Why, I don't know what need for freedom she has; she is a little nigger girl running off, that's all I know about her. Is it from Olaf that she runs or some other man? From too much work? Had Olaf in his drunken rage begun attacking her or beating her? I don't know. Was it that she loved Sims? I don't know even who he is. It is not that the girl has any hold on me that way, he thought. Is it some wish I have for her? I don't know. I don't think so. Not now, here at this time, certainly, yet here at this time I cannot leave her. She is a dirty, sick, scraggly girl who has bedeviled me, yet I cannot leave her. Why? August asked himself.

The wagon owner's wife, a heavy-set lady of about forty, was weeping, was claiming that these possessions were her inheritance. The men cared nothing for all that. They kicked open boxes of clothes and pots and books. They kicked open bags of flour and sugar and whatever else was available to them. They tore the tailgate from the wagon and threw that aside. They began to disassemble the wagon and sail its pieces across the field. Other men, thwarted by the absence of more merchandise, moved to other wagons and began to throw their goods onto the field, and farmers who tried to defend their possessions were shoved aside, even struck down. Several women began weeping, children were distraught, the confused dogs were barking at most everything, teams of horses were set free. A team broke through a shelter some poor farmer had built for his family, and went charging on toward the river, dragging his blankets after them like flags.

Whatever comes in the men's path now, August thought, will be split open down the middle.

His own cart was in their way. He started toward it, to save it. In his path a farmer pulled a black man from under a wagon and began to beat him; he was a young black about sixteen, about Anna's age. August saw two farmers grab another black man, one about twenty, and knock him to the ground, and a third man came running forward and with all his might kicked the black man in the stomach with his boot, a most brutal blow, hollow, cracking. August went on, wading through such sights, trying to get ahead of the tide of madness, pushing through the masculine, tribal odor of the place.

A man kicked an ox in the belly.

Two men knocked out of the way a white farmer who was trying to save his cart. They tore his cart's tailgate off. "Don't you run from me," one of them said to a black, "come help," and the three of them turned over the cart even as a boy tried to set it afire. Men were moving to August's cart now. "Turn it over," one of them said.

God knows, don't take to the woods, August told himself, don't be a fool, save her somehow, he said to himself. The two men turned toward him. To his own astonishment, he kicked his mare in the belly. The men grunted in pleasure. "I'll show you how to do it," he said, and kicked her again, and she, poor creature, lunged forward, started down through the field, the cart shuddering, bouncing over ruts and rocks, the sack of salt falling out, breaking open. August ran after the cart, past fires and little camps, through a drove of pigs, through a chicken flock, until far down the hillside he caught hold of the harness. Even so, the mare pulled him along for a ways, punishing him even further. He pleaded with her to stop, please stop and let him explain.

She stopped just past a brier thicket which had its way with him, and he tied her to a bush and embraced her neck and told her he was a fool and not to pay any attention to him. He told her she had always been dear to him, which was true, lord knows. Then he hurried to help Annalees get out from under the bags of goods. Her face was so strained with fear that he turned away from her, turned his own face from her, ashamed of all men like him, of all men unlike him, all born brutally.

He sat down near the cart, feeling like weeping, spent and empty, angry with God or devils for having permitted a caldron of this sort to be made, thankful to God for having saved him from its fires, annoyed to find himself thanking God or angels when he suspected they had enjoyed the sight, the spectacle, of this persecution and knew they had failed to intercede on his behalf.

Nobody else was near him, not way down here. A few pigs were rooting nearby. It will take a long time to get everything sorted out and put back together, he thought. "It rises like a storm and won't accept comfort," he told the girl, "won't allow appeasement. It has to ride itself out."

She moaned, a deep sound of mourning. "Did they kill him?" she said.

"I don't know what you mean," he said.

"Did they kill Sims?" she said.

"No," he said, meaning yes, they had killed him. "This wheel is doubtless worse," he said. "I wonder how many more journeys my cart will last. I can buy a wheel, but I'll need to save for it this next year."

"I heard them say—" she began.

"I'll have to buy a bag of salt from somebody, too," he said.

"They said they had killed him."

"Oh," he said, "they have all sorts of reports out here of late." She knows very well, he told himself. Why doesn't she admit she knows and stop asking me to tell her what she and I both know, even if neither of us can believe it yet.

She crept out of the wagon and urinated on the ground near him, then crawled back inside. It bothered him that she had been so blatantly immodest; she was an animal in most every way, apparently, which annoyed him. She could not have found a private place, it was true, not out here, but there certainly were more private places than beside him. You are saving a savage for freedom, August, he told himself. What is freedom to the savage?

Wagons now were following one another out onto the field, onto the road, way off. He saw Olaf's wagons pass. Far off he recognized the old Negro. He didn't see Olaf anywhere. The old Negro walked with his shoulders bent, his eyes gazing at the ground before him. He carried a weight of worry, August knew, and of wonder. He is the Hebrews' scapegoat in the desert, he thought. On him we will put our sins. If we did not have him, we would need to use one of ourselves, or my red boar or my young cow.

Somebody somewhere started picking out a song on his guitar. The player was in the field, in the midst of the broken possessions. A fiddler joined in. August couldn't see him. A fire flared up, made from the splintered wood of chests and wagons. This was directly up the hill from where he and Annalees were. He noticed that a few angry men came storming back along the line of wagons, saying, stop it, stop it, stop that noise. The music grated on their nerves, apparently.

The music continued, anyway, regardless of them. The musicians and their disciples were gathering now in strength.

One wagon after another was passing on, slowly along into the woods.

"We'll wait until the line is gone," he told Annalees, "and the road is clear from both directions."

Better to wait here, he thought, now that there is music. The music is washing the field. It is cutting down the anger like a sickle in ripe grain. See how other musicians gather and young people find places on the torn grass.

Oh, God knows, it is a pity to think of it all. Mankind is a dream only. It is two dreams, one following another. See the riders approaching the butchers' poles. See the young man standing on his horse's saddle. He cuts down one half of the body with one long slash of his knife. There is no laughter, not even at the awkwardness of the body as it crumples into a spongy pile; most unlike a body, for it folds at the ribs.

The young man cuts the other half down. Most unlike a body it falls.

The musicians are not noticing this, do not seem to notice. They merely glance that way, accepting it. They go on playing as the horse drags the halves of the body up into the woods above the field. How quickly, casually the young men work, the makers of music.

"We have no more fields to cross," he said to Annalees. He was sitting near the cart; he was leaning back against the left wheel of the cart, looking up across the littered field, and she was inside the cart. "From here the road is like a throat through the woods, with minor roads leading down to the valleys, to Hobbs, to Harristown. We'll be home tonight."

When she said nothing, he pushed himself warily to his feet and went around to the back of the cart and looked in at her. Her eyes were red, though not from weeping, her face was older by a long time of experiences, her mouth was slightly sunken, as if it had been devouring itself from inside.

"My dear girl," he said suddenly, and held out his hand to her, and with both her hands eagerly she grasped his hand and held it, held to it; her fingers dug deeply into his palms. She held to him and began to moan softly, deeply, a womanly sound, a plea of some sort, as she held to his white hand.

He was on the road again. He could hear the music for a while, then all he heard was the noise of the wind, which rustled past him and above him, through the yellow and red trees above his head. The trees grew to the road and overhung the road, so it was dusk in here now, even though he supposed the world was still bright outside. His mind ventured into new thoughts warily, changing often, seeking pain and seeking to avoid pain, refusing in any event to be to any subject long committed.

Had the girl actually seen the body? he wondered. Of course, she must know Sims was dead, yet she had accepted August's assurances that he was not. Which did she believe? She was whimpering and was drawn up in a knot, her knees close to her chin. Whenever he walked quite near the front of the cart, he could peek in and see her. Her eyes were open and were tearless, but he suspected she could not see or hear or feel anything.

She is a drugged child, he thought, she is my child, to be helped. Helping her is something that has fallen to me to do.

There was a white smudge on her face, where her damp skin had touched the flour bag.

What would she reply if he said, Did you love Sims? He would not ask her now, of course, he would not be so cruel as even to remind her of him. But what would she say? Why, what is love? Is love what I feel when I see my lover come in from the fields, his body bent from work and hopelessness and helplessness? Is love the sensation I feel of a night when I lie locked in my room and want somebody to soothe my loneliness? Is it the hunger I have, a need for somebody to be with me other than my mother? Or my father, whoever he is,

Olaf or some other? Or my brother or sister, whoever and how many of them there are?

Is love walking down to the spring and having the hands of a man come out to grab me, or of two men, my friends or my brothers or my friendly brothers? Is love fighting off the hands of men grabbing at me? Is it consenting near the river to the hands of a man and hearing him laugh as later he leaves me? Or two men laughing? "We got her that time."

Is love a want or desire; is it an adventure after a year of routine work and drudgery and weariness?

Is it fear of him, that he might suddenly straighten and strike me down, my father, if he is my father, my owner and my lord in any case?

Is it hope that I might flee and find a place away from here and from my mother and my father, whoever he might be, where I can breathe free of them and all the dread of childhood incidents?

Is love anguish?

Is it getting bigged?

Is it sympathy?

When white men say "love," what do they mean? What do you mean? What does a white woman mean? That she will have babies to care for? Meals to cook? Purposes to fulfill, morning, noon, evening, night, purposes to fulfill of her own? For all her life?

A house of her own.

But for me there is no purpose ever of my own.

For me there is nothing I own or ever will own. No thing. No husband, son, daughter will I own, either. No home.

So what is it you ask of me?

August said to her, "Does Olaf travel to his place on that Hobbs road or does he wait for the Harristown road?"

She said nothing.

"He lives between the two, so if he goes down through Hobbs, then we are done with him now, for that's the Hobbs road back by that big gray rock."

She said nothing.

"I think he might go that way, might have left us by now," August said, and a loneliness came over him and shivered through him and chilled his bones and flesh, so that he pulled his jacket closer about his neck. Was he disappointed, he wondered, that the danger was passing, that he was shedding the pursuers as he neared home? Was it conceivable that he wanted the chase to continue as before? "I want to get home," he said suddenly, affirming that need, which was as real and promising as any other.

Who gets the hide? he asked himself, the thought slashing through him.

"The hide was not unblemished," he told her.

Am I a priest? he asked. Am I ever to speak again at the church? My Jersey cow, should I have taken the hide? What is the hide of a black man, is it like a deer's? Can a coat be made of it to cover my white flesh? I will stand before my fellow Christians and say the water in the river is Jesus' blood.

His mind roved and roamed, darted here and there, pecking at pain, flirting with anger which was a clot in his chest, so that now and again he wanted to utter a scream against the horrors around him, and at the folly of his faith in mercy once he considered the pain men

153

cause, the blood they shed. "Sometimes I want to yell, Annalees," he said, "and I don't know what it is. Like those men at Buffer tore up wood, even."

She said nothing.

"Do you ever want to yell at the air?" he said. "That tree there—a bear will beat it, beat the bark, has to beat a tree, a male bear when it is mating season."

She was shivering in the cart. He saw her; he peeked in and saw her lying there, the bag of coffee pulled close to her belly as if it was a baby in her womb, her eyes open as if seeing her birth, her baby born, the bag of coffee born.

I was selected to take care of her, he told himself, say what you will. I was singled out. Whether by God or some other mystery I don't know, and whether for God's pleasure or by reason of his displeasure I don't know. Do I amuse him with my bungling? I wonder.

Colored leaves still sheltered them, some of them fell, twirling in the air, covering the road in this place, so that there were no tracks, making a soft carpet over the rocks.

"Can I sit up?" Annalees said.

"No, no, you stay down," he said. "Nothing is more unsettling to me than confidence. Used to Sarah would say, 'Let's spend at least two dollars on a mirror, instead of using that piece of one we got at home, please, August,' she would say, 'we can afford one luxury,' but I would say, 'Not now, Sarah, we must invest wisely what we have, every dollar we have, for there is no way to know what God has in store for us.'"

"My leg muscles have fire in them," Annalees said.

"You can exercise your legs when we get home.

We're near home now. An hour or two more is all. My lungs begin to breathe more air when I get near home, do yours? My chest expands, even my nostrils. I walk lighter." He saw that she lay with her face flat against the floorboard. "You're going to have bruises, as well as cuts and tears," he told her.

A misty rain began. How long the rain had been falling outside the leaf-protected world he walked in, he didn't know, but just now the first drops of rain fell on his face. "It's going to make these leaves slippery, I expect," he said.

How beautiful it is along this stretch of road, he thought. Why is the world not like this always? No dangers here at all, only soft colors and soft shapes and slowly changing shapes and slowly falling leaves and the gentle mist beyond the trees in those places where one can see beyond the trees or through them, the trunks of the oaks black with dampness. "A cart won't break," he told her, "it's not likely to break. A wagon is more likely. I could have traded my cart for a wagon several times on these journeys, but I recognized the dangers. It's more likely to break, and then, too, I can carry more goods in a wagon, so I will buy more goods, don't you see?"

For a while the girl slept. At least she had her eyes closed. She reminded him of his own baby being asleep. He recalled how angelic she looked. My baby was angelic, he thought.

Not so, not so, he thought, remembering the doctrine of his own church, even his own sermon on baptism.

Well, it seems to me she was, he thought.

The girl stirred in the cart, but remained asleep.

155

My girl, dear girl. What a happy girl you will be if I can get you safely through to evening. I will build a fire in my house and feed you properly. We will even have wine to drink. Dear girl.

He was moved to tears by a surge of affection for her. He had saved her. He suffered a delicious, tender compassion for her. He wanted to go on helping her forever. It came as near to love of her as he could come, not having known her long, not having known love either. She is perfect, he thought, whatever her faults.

Beautiful sunset. He could see glimmers of the western sky below the rain cloud, off through a forest of beech trees.

"Will it be dark when we arrive home?" she said.

"Yes, but never mind. The horse knows the way," he said.

"Do we have to pass many houses?"

"Two," he said. "The blacksmith's and the Plovers'. But they go inside early and shut their doors."

"I wish I was there," she said desperately.

"I will see you to it," he told her. "Not much have I ever promised in my life and not done. I promise you."

It was just as well the cow was gone. If the cow were still with him, he would have to stop and milk her, to relieve her of even the little bit of milk she gave. She had been a beautiful animal, he must admit; if he had kept her she would have been as good a cow as any James Turpin has. But he wouldn't be able to stop to milk her.

The geese were noisy, and that worried him. They would make even more of a fuss now that dark was coming, if they were denied a perch and quiet. They would refuse to consent to any peace at all, even though he begged them and Annalees pleaded with them.

"I recall there's a signal oak at the Harristown road. I remember when I first saw it. I was with Sarah, and she and I were friendly then, for we were just married. When we got to the oak we could see Harristown, which at that time was only a few houses and sheds."

Annalees got to her knees and held to the front sideboard of the cart.

"And I held Sarah, there at that oak. We hugged each other and did a dance. We seldom felt like that again. Except now, just now I feel it growing inside me, do you?"

"Can we see it yet?" she said.

"A minute or two more. Oh, my Lord, to think we have about got home, Anna."

It was a big red oak, a reddish brown color with massive limbs that shadowed the earth all around, for sixty, seventy feet on every side of its trunk, which itself was eight feet across. When he came in sight of it, he took the harness and pulled the horse forward. "Quicker, quicker," he said. When they came to the tree he stopped, awed by it, then awed by all below him, Harristown spread out in its valley below, being washed just now by the cool rain. Annalees stood up in the cart to see it. He caught hold of her and lifted her out and led her to the overlook and showed her the sight, the holy sight of it, and even embraced her, and she began to laugh, to squeal with delight as she wriggled free of him and climbed onto a big rock so she could see all of it better, the magic village below, thirty or more houses silvery of roof, each with sheds and barns and pens, all silvery of roof, the river more silvery than they. Here and there smoke was rising from a chimney, and he saw a cart, or maybe a sled, being pulled along one of the two river roads and a man walking, coatless, long-legged, his shoulders thrown back, his arms swinging freely. Mart Martingale, going home now after visiting at the mill, Mart Martingale who once had said to him, "Each man must go to the mill whose machinery he likes to hear run," which was a remarkable statement for him to say, for there was but one mill in Harristown, only one in any community that August knew about, just as there was no more than one of anything, and no more than one way for anything to be done in any one community.

"See there," August said huskily, "how pretty it is." And safe, he thought. No more danger here, for the Harristown road wound down to safety, he could see safety. He would go down to the little river, and cross the three creeks which joined to form the river, in clear sight below him half a mile away, and he would go on to the river road and turn right and go along that road, which became little more than a trail soon thereafter, and little more than a rutted cart path as it climbed the side of the ridge to his house.

He could see cattle standing in many fields. He could see old Mrs. Master's flock of sheep, as well as another flock, maybe James Tomlinson's. He didn't know. He was too excited to sort it all out. A community is a complex machinery which must fit in gear and belt, cranny and nook, each part with a name and a walk of its own type, and a road to its house, yet all along one river.

All governed by one mind, too.

"That's Mooney Wright's place," he said, pointing, "that big one that sprawls out, as if it's insisting on being comfortable. All those barns and sheds are his."

"Must have many slaves to help him tend all those fields."

"Not a one, except his sons, and those other men who need money or help of a sudden, they will often work for him; all of us, one time or another in our lives, are likely to be Mooney's slaves. It sounds unkind when I say it. But he is generous to a fault."

"You afraid of him?" she said, watching August closely.

He shrugged uncomfortably. "No more than anybody else is," he said.

She stood calmly beside him, her gaze roving over the magnificent river valley. "It's all beautiful as God's han'," she said.

He considered that for a moment. "Strange way to talk," he said.

"My mama is all the time talking about God's han'."

"Why?"

"I never as't her what she knows about it. Maybe she's been touched by it once."

"Doubt that," he said, and laughed softly, kindly. "Come along. We will go down there now," he told her, his body shivering with pride, "we'll go home now," he said, his voice trembling like the wind in the trees above them which guarded this place.

10 THE ROAD to the valley was steep. It had been cut by thirty years of use into the side of the ridge. Most all the time, as dark settled firmly on them, they could see the community below.

"We'll have a party at the house," he said to her, "the two of us, not the sort of party I used to have for myself alone. Listen, I have wine hid there, did I tell you?"

"Party for yourself alone?" she said.

"Sometimes I would, I would make myself the best food I could imagine and feast myself after Sarah died. I know it's strange."

She looked eagerly over the front of the cart at the firelighted chimneys, breathing their hot breaths into the air; she wasn't paying much attention to him.

"Take us a bath, get clean, have a feast," he said, "drink a toast to Olaf Singleterry, old what's-his-name himself, thinking we couldn't get through the net he set. Who says? Who says?"

"I know we've done it," she said happily.

"And that boy got through, too, take my word for it," he said, "that boy Sims is all right. I heard two men talking about it, how there had been a hundred rumors of his capture, but every time they went to see him the rumors proved false."

"I know Sims must be all right," she said. "He was like a cat with his lives, and he moved like a cat, with a limber step."

"And tomorrow I'll take you up to that northern trail—see it there, how it skirts the top of the ridge. Well, that top field over there is my field, and down below the field is my house. So it's not far, do you see?"

"I see it."

"It's all working out, I tell you. Though it has been a time, hasn't it, Anna?"

"I'll say it has. More'n I imagined it would be. Why, I only meant to free myself."

"But it'll be easier from here on. Few travel the northern trail you'll be on from here, and not many who do will know of any reward for you."

He was talking away in a loud, clear voice, quite unmindful of any danger at all, uncaring about the cold rain that was wetting him through to the skin. He didn't care about that one bit. "My wife, Sarah, and I made a bathing place in our creek," he said. "It's about three feet deep, has flat rocks on the floor of it. I'll wash the rain and mud off of me, before I go into the house. Might as well, for I'm soaked already."

Down the steep, narrow, slanted road to Harristown, darkness enfolding them, Annalees laughing now and then, a sound of happiness, soft musical sounds, she sitting up in the cart now, watching the red-mouthed chimneys grow closer in the night.

All perfect, except for the geese. The honking, miserably honking geese.

He stopped the cart and fussed at them. "Here, give me that piece of cow's rope," he said, and he tied the three geese with it, each by one leg, and led and carried and dragged them into the woods, the gander spitting at him, and tied the rope to a sapling. "Now you stay here till morning," he told them. "It's not long." Their wings beat at him, their beaks snapped at him. They were raising a terrible racket.

He stumbled back out to the cart and waited for a while in the rain, and only when they were quiet did he start on.

"They'll be all right," he said. "Geese are fierce. They can protect themselves from most anything. And tomorrow morning early I'll come for them. They'll be all right there."

He came to the three creeks which formed a web, which merged to make the head of the river. The third one of these creeks started as a spring up back of August's house. "You be steady in these little fords," he told his horse. The moon wasn't visible through the rain clouds, so it was darker than most nights, except when lightning flashed.

He stopped at the edge of the first creek. "It's not deep. It won't wash over the wheel hubs," he said. He walked through the creek, holding to the horse's harness; they splashed their way across.

Then he heard a horseman up ahead and stopped at once. Only the hoofs of a horse were heard for a few moments, and Annalees's breathing, a throaty breathing through her mouth.

A voice far off said, "I always get sleepy once it's dark."

The voice was the preacher's, and it came from beyond the third creek crossing, or so August guessed.

"We have no need to stay here all night," another man said.

A man said, "Some people are on the road, even yet."

"Who might be traveling after dark? No kin of a civilized man."

"A nigger will travel more at night than day. They see better of a night. Like a cat."

"Naw. Do they?"

"Like a cat. Ever see one walk, so soft and even and like a cat. Like that boy they caught. And they got cat's teeth."

"Where's the girl, that's what I want to know. We been trailing her for two days."

"Dangerous to this whole country. Never ought to have brought them in, but it was a favor done to them, to Christianize them."

August tied the horse's reins to a tree branch overhead and crept forward. Beyond the third creek he came in sight of a tiny fire, no bigger than a fist, or two fists held side by side, and hovering over it were four men, like hunched witches in the night, black bodies, warming their hands, speaking quietly one to another, the preacher holding the reins to his horse, a craggy man fresh from the Buffer field. Did he have blood on his coat, on his hands? Had blood splattered on his face? Reverent blood. The miller was there, a descendant of outlanders, not himself an owner of slaves but a hater of blacks, a quiverer before the mention of them. And with them stood the two lean hunters last seen at the creek at the Buffer field, seen before that in the Inn yard, both black silhouettes beside the glimmer of the fire. The fire fluttered its light around them in a circle, itself but little bigger than they, though the fire threw their shadows on the trees nearby and overhead.

"Rid this country of an illness before we're done," the miller said. "Pluck the mote from our eyes, pull the knife from our ribs before we die."

The preacher said, "It's hard, it's hard, God knows. They turn away from the truth. They admit to no moral laws."

"Don't have souls," a hunter said.

"Some say they do," the preacher said, "a nut of a soul. Nothing developed, as might be in a white man who has studied the Bible, who has loved God and hated the devil."

"That nigger they killed at the Buffer field—" a hunter said.

"Yes, I was there," the preacher said, "I heard him call out to God one time, as if he hoped God would know he was there. I saw him killed. A scared boy, not more'n a sack of meal by the time he called to God, Olaf facing him, the boy stammering answers, saying he knew where she was, then that he didn't know where she was, the ax swinging closer every time, big Charles Atkins wielding it."

"He can split a penny with an ax, I've heard," the miller said.

"The nigger giggling, gurgling out his answers, trying to admit to any guilt he could if it would save his life for even a minute longer."

"What value is a life to such as him?" a hunter said.

"I decided he never knew where the girl was," the preacher said, "for how would he know? Would a buck care about her, would he risk his own capture by caring for her? I think not. He can travel faster than she can, can go day and night. So he left her, and I said to Olaf, 'I imagine he left her near the start.' For they have not much soul, a butternut to an apple I expect, no tenderness in their natures, no spark of divinity such as we have, even after Adam's sin, for we are God's chosen, even so, the Jews first, then we who bless his name, Jesus' name, the lamb God slew, we slew for our sins, we are the chosen now, a people of itself, off to itself, with its own ways; we have an image of our divinity in the mirror of our former faces, we are not dead to God." As in a sermon he spoke, intoning some of the words, with breathy excesses, his breath like a whiplash flicking the air, his mind coasting on the melody of his own voice, his head moving rhythmically, his shoulders swaying so that his movements were reflected on the trees about him, behind him, and above him.

"It's colder'n creek water," the miller said. "I expect I'll go turn in. My wife's to home alone and she gets frightened on nights as dark as this, moonless, with the world unsettled. Come stay the night, Jacob?"

"No, I'm bound for Mooney's house," the preacher said. "My back's got so it likes his cot very well."

The two moved on together, the preacher's horse following, its hoofs clanking on the rocks of the road. The two hunters stood unchanged, unmoving, at the fire, warming their hands as before. The preacher began to sing as he walked away, his voice hoarse and raspy.

Down in yon forest be a hall,
Sing May, Queen May, Sing Mary. . .

August stood still as death, waiting for a sign of what he ought to do. He had lost his bearings on finding these two men waiting here. It never had been in his mind that he could fail in his own valley. He knew full well he could not. And he knew at this last moment he would not consent to losing all he had gained, not to them especially, the two hunters, to their cold eyes and steady hands and unrelenting ways.

He crept back to his cart, quietly made his way to the tailgate and whispered to Annalees, "We'll go on foot from here." In the dark he couldn't see her. He reached out and touched her, felt her head, let his fingers rest for a moment against her face. "Now, now," he said. Groping for her with his hands, he caught her arm and helped her, lifted her in his two hands and quietly set her on the ground. He led her into the woods, carefully into the thick woods, feeling his way along from one tree to another.

There was no sound from the direction of the fire, from the two hunters. There was not even the sound of the hunters' voices. They have nothing to say to one another, he thought.

Step by step, slowly, they made their way through a stand of hemlock trees and reached the road, then moved to the right along that road. "It's all well now," he told her. "We've got through," he said, and sighed, comforting and congratulating himself, and began to hurry, stumbling awkwardly, for there was no moonlight at all.

"Ghosts travel on nights," she said, meaning on nights like this.

The road became a trail. He was still holding her hand. They passed the German's house. Rainwater was falling from his porch eaves. A lamp was lit in his main room. "The German might help us, if we need help," he told her, "though he would debate it with himself for hours first." He didn't want the German to help. He didn't want to share her company.

They stopped at the lower fence to August's own property while he moved the split rails out of the way, then replaced them to keep the cattle in.

"I got this swimming place," he told her, "though I don't swim. I can swim, but I don't, not so much as I stand or sit in the water."

Her teeth were chattering.

"You want to see it?" he said.

"No," she said, moaning.

"I won't be long," he said. He led the way down a rocky path to where the water sounded vigorous and churning as it splashed into the little pool. He knelt beside the pool and put his hands and arms into the water. Shivers of pain went through them. "I like pain better'n pleasure, don't you?" He laughed. "Lord knows, it begins to warm." He pushed himself on into the water, clothes and all, and the sting of the coldness burned his skin and sparked like a thousand needles through him. "Ayyyyyy!" he cried. "Ayyyyyyy, Lord knows," he said, tears coating his eyes. He crouched, so that the water came up to his chin—it was only three feet deep, not even that deep. "Ayyyyyyy."

"They hear you?" she asked.

"No, not up here. Nobody up here," he said. "Come in here, Annalees."

Her teeth chattered. "No," she said.

"Shove yourself off that rock you're squatting on."

"It's cold, I imagine," she said.

"Law, you telling me and me standing in it?" he said. "But it warms you. What's cold will warm you. You come on and see."

He heard her push herself off the rock and into the water, and at once she began to gasp and squeal.

"What you think of it?" he said.

"Oh, mama," she said huskily, gasping for breath.

"It'll close your wounds," he said.

"It'll kill me," she said, gasping.

"Well, it might," he said. "Sarah said it was cold."

"Cold?" she gasped. "Cold?"

"Well, I know," he said, feeling warm now, the cold water comforting him, the water cleansing him. "Ahhhhhhh," he moaned. "In here even Sarah wouldn't ask why."

A touch of moonlight. A tiny break in the clouds no larger than a thread. A moment of light and he saw her lift her head and throw the water back off her hair, her two hands pressing against her face, her eyes closed. Then in darkness he heard her moan. Later, in amid the splashing that he heard, was a tinkling, friendly laugh, to say she was comfortable, was friendly to the water and the pool and even to the splattering, soft rain falling on the two of them, close together. She giggled, a soft sound, mingling with the noises of the creek.

"I been here many a time," he said, "though only twice before of a night. I was burning the field on those

168

two times, burning stumps and brush, and I had to tend the fire until after dark, and I was hot and grubby and smoked and dry, so I came here those two nights and Sarah crouched on that rock and advised me that I was a fool for this world."

"We're crazy, I expect," she said, moaning with pleasure.

"I expect so," he said. "I never been through so much danger, have you?"

"Law, no, nor been so cramped."

"It'll wash us clean and close our pores. Why not be crazy, after a crazy day," he said, "if it warms you so well?"

She laughed and said she knew it was so. "I never been swimming like this before," she said. "I'm warm all through now. Makes me drowsy."

"Not now," he said, "we got the evening yet."

A flutter of light came in the sky. She turned, startled. "Who's that?" she said.

"Angels lighting lamps," he said.

"Why, it's breaking through," she said.

"Maybe we can see the path going home," he said. "I want you to see my house, Anna," he said. "You want to come with me now?"

The storm clouds parted as they climbed the trail. The moon shone brightly on the drops of rain which dotted the leaves and rocks. His spent cornstalks stood like jeweled spears, welcoming them, and beyond the cornfield was the house itself, which was shiny and beckoning, silver and luminous, and which was beautiful to him. He stopped on the trail itself, overcome to have reached this sanctuary, and stood there marveling that this earthen, log, stick, and rock house, that barn, that shed, that crib, those pens down there where the swine were, that long snake fence disappearing up the hill, could move him to tears by welcoming him to itself. He had constructed all of it, his own welcome and security.

"What you praying for?" she asked him.

"It's a miracle is all," he said.

"Praying for a miracle?" she said.

"No, it is a miracle. It is, we are," he said.

"Ahhh," she said, and made sighs and murmurs of consent.

He knew she was by nature wary of mysteries, even in conversation, but he supposed her life just now, the situation around her, seemed to have kindness to it. "I made all that," he said, but then he laughed at what he had said. "Only the buildings," he said, for looming high about them, over all of it, were the flanks and hoary crests of the mountains themselves, and all he had made were merely specks on the face of the earth compared to them, and above the mountains the moon-lighted sky rose and yawned. His small house, crib, barn, the clearing he had made with ax and fire were intimate and small and confining.

They approached the place together, his place and rock step, his porch and roof, his chair and door. God knows he loved it all. In the moonlight, after the rain, it all seemed to glimmer and vibrate as with a personal, inner spirit. He grabbed up a handful of pine kindling from the porch, the best of his lightwood, and fiddled with the latch, the wooden latch he and Sarah had made, for they had not wanted to use their money to buy a metal one. He pushed open the door he and Sarah had fitted and pegged and went inside the house they had raised, the girl lingering back a ways, watchful, suspicious of it all, of the darkness, perhaps of the ghosts that might be there, or hunters waiting for her, for them. He walked into the heavy, herby, root-intoxicating air of his room and crouched before the fireplace and lit the wood. At once its resin caught, the wood flared into light. "Come on inside," he told her. "It's all right."

She came just inside the door and looked around, as the red flicker of fire began to reflect from the log walls and the gray sapling rafters. From the porch he brought in three limb-logs of poplar which he had cut in the spring, and set them in the fireplace on the fire rocks he and Sarah had arranged. The eager fire bit at the poplar, the room burst into light, and he turned to look into the heart of the room, where his possessions were hanging from the walls and from rafters, and at her, she standing even now by the door as if ready to bolt into the yard and flee toward that northern trail up top of his ridge, dripping creek and rainwater from her hair and soggy dress, which clung to her young body, showing every curve and bulge and depression and nipple and even many of the scars on it.

She smiled at him suddenly, warmed by his own enthusiasm as well as by her own and by the sight and feel of the fire. She smiled warmly at the room, even as she stood there shivering from the wet. He snatched a piece of linsey from a stob on the wall and gave it to her to dry with, and he got another one from the drawered chest for himself. They dried their hair and faces, both of them stomping their feet and shaking off water, approaching the fireplace as close as they could, coming close to each other at the fireplace, both coughing out the cold air, breathing in the warmth, accepting it in their nostrils and mouths and the pores of their skin, increasingly alive in every part and aspect of their bodies to the sensations of warmth and dryness, and to relief and exuberance, which was in them, expanding inside them, ripening.

Abruptly he took his towel and rubbed her head with it, rubbed it firmly, and she began to giggle and laugh; he rubbed it all the harder to make her laugh all the more. "Crazy girl, you're a crazy girl," he said happily. He rubbed her shoulders, then her back, but when his hand touched one of her breasts, even by chance, she pulled away sharply, swung away from him, the laughter stopping and even the smile vanished, and a haunted, resentful look came into her eyes, almost frightening in its intensity.

He was not awkward or apologetic, even so. He faced her fairly, watched her, in the moment of her embarrassment and resentment. For a while, a long moment, they stared at each other, she defiantly, he questioningly, before she began once more to dry herself, to rub her thighs and legs with the linsey cloth, guarded even then, as he could tell, resentful even then, though she pretended casualness. "How far that trail from here? Up top your field, you said?"

"I never would want to harm a person," he said.

She went on drying. She threw her head back suddenly and began rubbing her hair briskly, rubbing it hard with the towel. "Ah, go on now," she said.

"I suppose it gets desperate—" he began, but didn't continue with it, didn't want to delve into the life she was trying to escape. "I won't bother you," he said.

"She's here," she said suddenly.

"Who?"

"Your wife."

"Oh, no, she's not. Sarah never liked this place all that much," he said, trying to joke about it.

"She's here," she said, and abruptly crouched before the fire, seeking greater warmth and protection from it, leaning close to the fire, baking her face and shoulders with the heat of it. And the redness of the fire made her bronze-colored skin shine like a clay-molding, one of a kneeling figure with beautiful arms, a thin waist and round hips, her legs folded under her gracefully.

She smiled up at him suddenly. "Sometimes my mama lets me wear her other dress while mine dries, but hers is way too round for me, and I look like a mushroom."

"Pretty mushroom," he said.

The smile vanished slowly and she turned once more to the fire. "I s'pose."

He had dry clothes for himself, anyway. He got out a shirt and pair of pants, and, while she watched the fire, put them on. He found another shirt in the drawer and tossed it to her. "It's something like a dress," he said.

She was interested enough to drag it close to the fire to judge its texture and color. She pressed it against her face. "It's a hard cloth," she said. She held it up to judge its size.

173

"Sarah made it out of linsey she traded Mrs. Wright for," he said.

"Pretty dye," she said. She unbuttoned her own dress at the front and wriggled her shoulders out of it. Even as he watched she let it fall around her waist. Without hurry she dried her naked chest and stomach with the cloth he had given her. She put the shirt on, considering the colors of it again, considering her own arm with the sleeve of the shirt on it. She buttoned the shirt, moving her arms and hands with a newfound pride and grace, as if she were a princess of some country putting on her royal garb.

She stood before the fire and turned so that the fire reflected in different patterns on the old shirt, which fell halfway down her thighs. She untied her dress belt under the shirt and her soggy dress fell around her feet.

All this he watched, trembling, his mind jarred by twisty thoughts he could not bear to accept or set aside.

11 HE HAD A FAT HEN. He killed it in the yard and let it flop about out there, then plucked it on the porch while it was warm. "There's no salt left in the gourd," he said, "but we can soak the gourd and make a brine water from it."

She milked the cow, she got a cup or two of milk.

"That German's wife milked her earlier," he said. "Not that the cow ever gives much, mind you. She's too irritable and old for it."

They took the milk and chicken indoors and used some of the milk to soak the gourd.

"That chest of drawers I made of cherry wood, Annalees," he said. "I let the wood cure a year. Sarah waxed the slides most every month, waxed them so often I've not needed to wax them since she died. Those are Sarah's clothes and things packed away in the top drawer, like she left them."

"I never thought you liked her so well," Annalees said, staring enviously, suspiciously at the piles of dresses and petticoats and gowns.

"That first year, or two years, we got along well,

175

before I began to resent her being here." The thought caught him unawares, for he had not known he had felt that way. He wondered what he had meant.

"She's still here, seems to me," she said, and she made a nervous gesture with her arms, a cross, warding off evil, which amused him, and he laughed, not at her so much as at how astonishing her worries were to him.

"She's way off from here. She has gone home, I suspect."

"Her clothes are not."

"Well, her clothes are no bother," he said.

There was nothing in the girl's manner to indicate that she wanted the clothes for herself, and even when she had been soppy wet he had not thought of letting her wear one of Sarah's dresses. The thought did come to him now. Sarah had three left here, other than the white one he had buried her in, including her blue dress which he liked especially well. He was on the verge of suggesting Annalees might want to put it on, but instinctively he turned from that idea, not because of what reaction he feared she would give but because of doubt in his own mind. There was a secret crevice or two there which he had not explored, had not even known about until this moment, while he was standing near the girl before the open chest of drawers, and he drew back from it.

The girl was distracted by the mirror, or what she thought was a mirror. It was a window with four panes of glass. He drew the curtain back all the way, and she came close as her breath to it and felt of it, ran her fingers along the sweaty panes of it. "Law, he's got a hundred panes of glass in his house," she said.

Now, he believed she wasn't trying to hurt him, that she was only trying to protect herself from him, and from this room, which had become inviting and warm and was comfortable and was even comforting, which felt homelike, and which was where he and she were alone. "I know he's rich as the world is round," he said.

"He has glass windows in every room of his house, and two windows in the parlor." She crouched before the window, smiling at her reflection. She smiled up at him. "I see myself," she said.

"Not a scared girl, either," he said, "not any longer."

She frowned, even as she looked at him. "I wasn't scared," she said.

He crouched beside her, touched her hand sympathetically. "You're such a young girl, you made me feel old a while ago. You mean to hurt me, do you?"

"I don't know," she said. "How old you?" Her hand came up to touch his face, but as she touched his skin, the merest whisper of a touch, a frown of bafflement came over her face. "Ahhhhh, no," she said, and drew away from him quickly, leaving him kneeling there.

He showed her where he had cut the marks into the floorboards to make the sun clock. Some of them had filled with dirt, and with her fingers she cleaned them out carefully.

"We made this floor together, Sarah and me. We cut down an oak, which is a heavy chore, on the old of the moon, and in summer so the bark would come off by itself. We split the floorboards off of it. We cured the joists up off the ground until they were bone hard, and we jointed them to the sleepers using four-foot centers.

We borrowed tools from four different families—a broadax, foot adz, a froe and mallet, a maul, an auger and got a drawing knife from the preacher. Well, Sarah and I did all of it. We had no wealth to buy help back then. We did it, and it took most of a winter to finish. Then here I came later with a knife and gouged out holes on the floor, and naturally she said, 'August, you can't do that to my floor,' which made me angry, saying I couldn't do so and so to my own floor. This is my house, after all, this is my farm. If it was hers, why did she resent it so much? She couldn't go visit her people, she said. Well, her mother was an unfeeling person, in my opinion, and her father couldn't hear even a yell. She had no friends up here, she said, except the Germans, and Mina never had anything to say to her except what the omens were. So . . ." He hesitated, looked about frustratedly. "I don't know what I was telling, do you?"

"About the notches in the floor."

"Oh, it doesn't matter," he said. Lord, what does it matter, he thought, why tell this girl about all that, about Sarah and how he had set her aside, to one side, as he went on with his life. "I know I should have said, 'Look, Sarah, we ought to go see your people for a month.' We could have. We did have a good start, even by the fifth year."

"You build these walls?"

"I get wrought up, thinking about Sarah. I wish I could argue it out with her, don't you know, to make myself clear, but I never got a chance."

"You and her?"

"Yes, we argued, but not about this, the—"

"You build the walls?"

"Oh, yes, though we had help from the German. Not much help though, for he's not much help with his hands. He's a thinker and a complainer. He can think and complain about most anything. But if you don't agree with him, he goes into a pout. So I agree with him ordinarily. His own wife, well, they don't speak very often to each other, for she won't always abide his opinions, either."

"How long did the logs have to cure?" she said.

"We used poplar and chestnut, so it didn't take long. If we had used oak, we never would have got it done, don't you know, not that first year. We used oak sleepers, and when we made the porch, we used oak."

"How many years were you here without a porch?" she said.

"I don't know. Five or six."

She wandered over to the west wall, where she examined the things he and Sarah had saved over the years. A chain. Two pieces of rope. An extra plowpoint. A hoe. A froe. A long knife with one handle missing just now. A rocker for a chair—he had not carved the other one yet. A batch of leather thongs. An iron lock that he had found on the valley road. It had no key. Four nails, not enough for a door, not enough for anything really, not enough for a coffin, not enough for a table, if one was going to use nails in a table to start with. His old gun.

"Your powder horn's empty," she said.

"I have more powder in the cart," he said.

"What's all these bags for?" she said, moving to the adjoining wall, where he and Sarah had put shelves.

"Well, I tell you, Sarah knew herbs and roots and

bark the best you ever saw. She gathered all those medicines, and I helped her."

"I never saw such a lot."

"Oh, she was the best hand in the world for healing. That bottle you have in your hand is a salve she made from bee balm and mutton tallow." He read aloud some of the labels on the jars: cherry bark, cherry root, yellowroot, sassafras, boneset, snakeroot, blackberry root, ginseng root . . . There were fifty or sixty different herbs in all. "So when she had a baby to worry about, she got to doctoring it for most every sigh, scared to death she didn't know enough to cure it properly, and when it did get an affliction, something or other, I don't know what, and began to frail and dissipate and even got blood in its bowels, as if something was inside there chewing on it, you know, and I—shivered sometimes, like she did, I mean I cried I did. I've not cried since, but I cried then, and Sarah made all sorts of damn teas and poultices and sops. And the baby coughed, got to coughing. I said to her that the cough wasn't what it was, wasn't the ailment, that there was a damn something inside the baby eating at its guts. Sarah kept trying to kill it, whatever it was, and she made some damn strong medicines, so that I would come in here and I could scarcely breathe the air, and the steam would rise from the pots like witches' brew. And I said, 'Let's take her to see what a doctor says,' and Sarah said it's too late to travel. And so it was, so it was, for you could hold the German's silver watch before my baby's nose and there was no mist formed by its breathing. And Sarah said, 'Oh, you brought me up here to this wild place,' and I said, 'Sarah, don't blame me, please don't blame me for it.' Why did she have to blame me for it?"

She stood staring at him, most mournful in her face, sympathetically staring at him with her head tilted slightly to one side, evaluating him. "So it died," she said.

"Oh, yes, the baby died," he said. "And when you come to it, that's why a year and a half later Sarah killed herself." He stopped, stone cold, sobered by his own words.

"She killed herself?" Annalees said, surprised.

"Why do you say she killed herself?" he said.

"You said it," she said.

"I don't remember ever saying it before," he said. He went over to the fire and crouched before it and poked at the logs. "Somebody used to say that. I've heard it said."

"But you said it yourself, don't you know that?" she said, crouching near him.

"Of course, I prayed. I used to promise God most anything, but he was deaf to me. I've not had the same feeling toward God since then. I never said that to anybody else, do you know it? I tell you, it's all right as a young man to love God and do his bidding, but you come up against a situation like that, with your baby bleeding inside, believing God could save her, knowing you've not sinned one damn bit, nothing to justify any such persecution as this, and you pray. I called out to God, I beat my head on the ground out there, and I said, 'God, do this for me and I will do for you whatever you say, long as I live, for Jesus' sake, A-men.'"

His voice had grown into a sob even as he talked,

but she was not offended by it; she accepted a show of emotion naturally.

"God giveth and God taketh away," he said. "Law, law," he said fitfully, trying to clear his mind of all of it, wondering how he had got started on it anyway. "Look here, you can use that black pot to cook the chicken in," he said.

She did feel sympathy for him, he could tell that. She was capable of sympathy. She had remained attentive to him, watchful of him as he spoke. Even now she watched him, glancing at him approvingly now and then, always calmly, as she wiped the pot clean with her hand and blew the dust out of it. "You have any oak or hickory to cook with?" she said.

He brought the wood in, then gave the salt gourd to her and she dampened the chicken with the brine. She greased the pot and set the chicken in it.

"Why did you run off?" he said.

"They were always trying to hurt me," she said, "since I lived in his house and had his favor. I used to say he's not my father in my opinion, but they had their own ideas about it."

"He's not your father, Anna?"

"My mama says my father was a white man on the road who told her to go into the woods, so she had to do it."

"Does your mother believe that you're not his child?"

"She says I couldn't be, that she wasn't even met by him for a full twelve months before I was born."

"Nine months, that's all a birthing takes," he said.

She flared up angrily. "You say what time you want to and I'll say what I want to," she said firmly. "I do

182

know some things for myself." She shoved the pot in among the coals, obviously angry.

He saw she was looking around for the pot lid, so he pushed it to her with his foot. She dusted it with her hand, blew dirt off of it and set it over the chicken, then covered the lid with hot coals, using a wooden shovel.

"I'm not stupid," she said suddenly. "One thing I don't like about white people is they never give me credit for knowing nothing."

They sat before the fire, the chicken cooking, and drank wine which he had made that summer from fox grapes. "I have some salve," he said, "if you want to put it on those cuts."

"I wouldn't mind," she said.

"Some Sarah made." He got the biggest pot of it. "In the Bible this is called balm of Gilead. Sarah had me climb a tree, I went to the top in winter to get the buds she ground. Here, take a handful. Or you want me to do it on your face first?"

"Yes," she said.

He rubbed salve into the cuts on her face. "You have a pretty face," he told her, "well formed features on you."

"I wonder if I do," she said.

"Look here on your neck, those cuts, like somebody with long fingernails snagged you."

"You shouldn't use your first finger to salve with. It's bad luck," she said.

She unbuttoned her shirt at the top, pushing it down over her shoulders. He salved her shoulders. When she let the shirt fall down around her waist, he continued

183

to rub the salve into her shoulders. He noticed that she was breathing more heavily than usual, as he was, and he wondered what he ought to do, what somehow he could bring himself to do, for he was attracted by a natural snare, one which embarrassed, even annoyed him grievously. His hand began trembling so much that he had to stop. He sat looking at the fire while she salved her own chest and breasts and stomach, and pulled the shirt back up into place, over her shoulders, not bothering to button it. She didn't salve her legs.

Maybe she is waiting for me to do it, he thought, caught in a storm of emotions he could scarcely control, feeling guilty and frustrated, for she was young and pretty and he and she had been through much danger together, and now they were dry and warm and were wine-dizzy and were waiting together.

He got up suddenly and without a word went out onto the porch and let the cold air sweep over him. He kept looking back at the girl, kneeling before the fire, turning the chicken in the pot. He watched her as she began rubbing salve into the cuts on her arms. Anxiously, guiltily he watched her, a passion growing in him which threatened to overcome him. He tore himself free of the sight of her and, frightened, moved toward the field, walking into his own rail fence, knocking two rails off of it, ignoring them.

Nigger, nigger in the night, he thought.

The little grave where the baby lay, he came upon it. He had covered it over with a large, flat stone soon after she was buried, after he had found a fox digging into it one morning. Nearby was Sarah's grave. He had often talked to the graves in his loneliness, and he talked to them now, though his mind ventured again and again to the girl and the open, red doorway of his house. She is the black tongue in the red mouth of my house, he thought, waiting to sting me with a lifetime sin. "Sarah, let me tell you about my journey," he said, his mind on the girl.

He told Sarah nothing about the girl, only about the journey, not even that he had found her in the woods. All the while he could see the girl moving before the fire. Her shadow flitted and played across the doorway, falling onto the porch, even onto the yard, even onto the barn, the side of the barn, even onto the hillside where he saw the shadow moving even across the graves and across his hands as he sought to touch it.

He talked about his journey, telling about the red boar he had bought and how he had gone in debt to buy him, all the while telling himself what God in Heaven and his own senses told him he would not do or try to do to the black girl, or try to do with her regardless of what she would permit, what in any case she would expect, asking himself if he was to become like the men in the field who would have raped her, was he fashioned in their image? Could he deny that he was? Did he deny that he wanted Olaf's daughter? Did he want to be Olaf the father? The lover in my own bed, he thought, in my own bed, in Sarah's bed, to rid that bed, on the floor of the house Sarah and I made—

Well, God knows he would not. He would not. He would not corrode what he had achieved. With kindness he had got her through the nets the other men had thrown for her, the common men who would have taken her, who would indeed have taken her to the ground, to a riverbank, to a pad of leaves, to a wagon. He would not dissolve, distress the strength of his own achievement. I cannot. God has a sense of irony, he thought, to put me in this place with her. Who else has such a mind? Did I bring her here? Does Mr. Wright have a mind like God's? Does the German? Who puts her there in the doorway of my house, red like the entry to a womb in which a black tongue moves, waiting to sting me?

He went down through the field, stumbling over his own spring rocks. Surely after eight years he knew they were there. Had he forgot them on this one night? He saw that the cow was not properly shedded. The shed door was standing open. The chicken door was open. What do you mean, August, leaving them open?

He stumbled on toward the house.

Where is she?

Three of his heifers waited by the fence. Put the top rails back now, he thought, but he did not stop. The cattle had come down from the top of the field to see the firelight at the door.

I must shut that door, he thought, moving to the porch, not remembering where the porch step was, making his way onto the porch and across the porch, shutting the door. He stood looking down at her, she sitting on the floor, glancing up at him, a wistful, child-like smile on her face which slowly closed when she saw his face. From the chest, from the top drawer, from the bottom of the stack of Sarah's clothes, he took the blue dress and brought it to her, and she didn't look up at him now, nor did she eagerly accept the dress, but she touched it, tentatively, cautiously touched it, felt the texture of the material, then her hand closed on it. She held it in her hands for a moment before she brought it to her face and touched her face with it. Then she held it forward into the firelight so that she could judge its color.

He tore himself away. No, by God, he would not. He moved out the door, he forced himself to leave her, and he crossed the yard and ran into the fence. He whacked it cruelly with his hand. Then he sank down, his face to the fence, to the two poles remaining in place.

He could see the girl before the fireplace. He watched trembling as she dropped the shirt from her body, let it fall to the floor. She stood naked before the fire. She bent over to pick up the blue dress from the floor. A graceful creature, he thought, a beautiful child-woman, a clean and beautiful, mature woman.

He would not look. He covered his face with his hands. He would not look any longer. I will put out my eyes, he thought. I will not look again.

Yet he peeked at her. Through the fingers of his hands he peeked at her. Through his own hands, holding up his hands as if they offered him a shield, he peeked at her.

Then once when he looked, when he peeked shamefully, shamelessly, she was gone. She was not there any longer. She had fled. Stiffly, breathlessly he moved toward the door, groping his way along, having forgot the path across his yard. He made his way onto the porch and gropingly to the door.

She was on the far side of the room, standing near the chest. She had been going through Sarah's things, that was all. She had put on the cheap bead necklace. She had put on Sarah's glass-jeweled comb, had stuck it in her own hair. Sarah's blue dress, which was too long for her, gathered in folds at her feet; she had not yet taken the trouble to button it, so it fell loose around her shoulders and gapped open at her chest. She was dressed as if for a ghostly dance, for a ghoulish ceremony—how absurd to see Sarah dressed so, with her comb about to fall out of her hair, with her necklace laid against her naked chest, between two firm, brown breasts.

"Ahhhhhhhhh," he said, and held out his arms to her, and went to her and took her into his arms, laughing, holding her, grappling for her as she wriggled in his arms to keep the dress from tearing—

"You're standing on my dress—"

Fondling her, giving way to her, to himself, groping for her body, she trying to keep him from breaking the necklace, asking him in a little child's voice please do not break my necklace, please do not knock the comb out of my hair.

He began to laugh. He could not help himself, could not keep from laughing.

"You knock my comb out my hair, I'll—"

"Your hair," he said, laughing, and he picked her up in his arms and whirled about the room with her, she complaining, then set her down again and went out onto the porch, snickering when he looked into the room and saw her trying to retrieve her comb from under the bed, then getting to her feet, adjusting her dress, trying to smile at him, apparently feeling that she must smile at him, a black Sarah smiling at him, so that he had to laugh and he sank down onto the porch, drunk with relief. "I don't even need you any more," he said.

12 IT WAS IN THE NIGHT that he led her to the trail top of his field, and they saw dawn come there. They had finished most of a gallon jug of wine and had devoured all the chicken, so they were full and were drunkenly happy, holding to one another for guidance and support. She had most all of Sarah's clothes, even the shoes, which were way too big for her but she wanted them anyway, and she carried a twelve-pound ham which had been cured and smoked, the last one August had left, and she had all his matches and had his best pot, so she could cook the ham for herself on the way to the promised land up there somewhere, off somewhere. "Mostly in your dreams, I expect," he told her.

"Golden streets," she said.

"Oh, yes, oh, yes," he said.

"I'll see Sims there," she said.

They got to the trail. It lay along the ridgecrest, wound about and around, meandering, finding its own way comfortably. There was no danger to it, not that the eye could see; here was a leafy path that nobody much had been on recently, for there were no ruts in

189

it. "Nobody been through since yesterday's rain," he said. Yet he wondered if she could ever reach the North. "You'll very likely fail a time or two, get so tired and sick you want to give up, but you need to remember that it is up there, Anna. Think how much progress you've made, you've come all this way."

"All these clothes," she said.

She still had that comb stuck in her hair, and it looked ever so strange to him. She had the blue dress on, even though it dragged the ground. "Well, you're tough, you're tough as can be. You go on now," he said, and he took her in his arms and held her, and she put her arms around him and squeezed him suddenly, then released him and got her pot and the ham, took one in each hand. "Those clothes packed all right?" she said.

"Yes, and the shoes," he said, checking to see that the pack was secure enough. "You go on, honey," he said.

She walked a ways, but stopped and turned to look at him, a longing look really, as if maybe she didn't want to leave.

"Oh, now, go on," he said. "I've got no more time for you," he said gruffly.

She turned and went on to the curve of the path, where she stopped again and turned to look at him, to wave at him.

"All right," he said, "you're all right. It's up there somewhere," he said.

She held her hand, one brown hand, near her face, so he raised his hand to her, then turned and left her, deciding he ought to help her leave by leaving her. And when he stopped finally and looked back, she was gone, there was nothing on the path at all except the colored trees along it and the colored leaves over it, and that was when he felt the loneliness for her settle on him and he began to cry.

Sometime later, there even yet, he wondered: Did Olaf feel such pain? Was it the same pain? Was it a love for her, or a love of owning her? Was it her company? Was it a spirit inside himself which needed to answer a calling, and she had been a part of that calling? In the October shadow of his life had he heard a calling?

Was a calling a new song, or an old one?

"Oh, God knows," he whispered, there at the top of his own field, which he and Sarah had hacked clear, had grubbed, burned over. "God knows," he whispered to the ground at his face. "I never loved her."

Yet something in him had been ripped open, so that his soul bled. The spear was in his own side now. "Oh, Jesus," he whispered, and lay as close to the ground, pressed himself as close to the ground as he could, wanting to be in it, in it, in it, comforted.

He sat in the sun, once it was high enough. The sun was from the morning-side and seemed to call him— not the light so much as the warmth. It asked him to be born for the day. The sun is cleansing. No, that's not true. The heat of the sun is cleansing, especially on an autumn day, or a spring day, when the air is cool. The warmth caresses not only the skin but also the body as a whole, it forms a membrane around it, as in a mother's womb.

He looked up into the light, into the heat, and after a while he got up languidly, carefully, so as not to break the spell he was under, he was in, and he stretched, feeling life, his own stirring, and slowly he allowed himself a luxury, one he had not allowed himself since Sarah died, since before Sarah died—how long ago since he had raised his arms into the heat of a morning sun and had said to himself, "August, you have done well."

EPILOGUE

HE WENT HOME in mid-morning thinking he would fetch his cart and supplies and see to his geese. He knew he had these chores to do, but he hung around the house and the yard, nostalgically walking about from place to place, thinking about the events of the past two days and of the girl, and of what he and Sarah had built, remembering the days of work specifically, so that the logs of the crib reminded him of a time, a certain time, when they had been laid. He went into his house and tidied up, folded the quilt which he had thrown over her once she had gone to sleep before the fire.

He was inside the house when he heard footsteps outside. "Mina?" he called. "That you? Who is it?"

Felix, the German, came inside, a small, neatly featured man in his mid-forties, sniffing and coughing and looking grave. He saw the dresser drawers open and empty, saw the dirty plates on the table, with the two chairs set one to a side. He cleared his throat importantly a time or two as if revealing the workings of a heavy mind. "Well, they found your cart," he said.

"Found my cart?" August said, astonished.

"It's nigh to Hobbs," Felix said.

"Hobbs?" August said. "Why, it's not, either."

"Its wheel is broke and it's parked in a gutter, off to one side."

"I left it with the mare at the creeks—"

"No horse," Felix said. "There's no horse at all."

"Well, where's Ophelia?"

The German mulled that over, squinting, his lips pursed. "Mina came up to milk and she couldn't find your old cow," he said.

"Why, the cow's outside."

"And what went with your chickens?"

"They're in the chicken house, where they are supposed to be."

"No, they're not there. And your cattle have strayed."

"Ahhhhhhh," August said, confused beyond reason by the deadening weight. "Are you saying my mare is gone?"

The German was studying him strangely, staring into his eyes as if to judge his temper.

"My cart is broke, you say?" August said.

"Yes, the cart is broke, the mare is gone—"

"The cart's not empty of the supplies, is it?"

"Why, there's nothing in the cart," he said.

And the geese, what of my geese, August thought, knowing they were gone by now, realizing it was all gone, taken away in a day's time, lost by him without anybody's aid, without Sarah or anybody's advice, by himself only, and a sense of astonishment came over him.

Felix came by again that morning, his wife Mina with him, a man and a fading woman, once pretty, who protected herself with silence, deferring always to her husband now that she was losing her attractiveness to him. The two of them, as August realized, kept watching him strangely. Anything he said, even a moan or groan out of his misery and confusion, would cause Felix to nod knowingly to her. Neither would come close to him, either, he realized, any more than they would have gone close to a man thought to be possessed of evil spirits, for such spirits can move from one body to another on skin-to-skin contact, the merest touch of bare flesh.

Later that afternoon, when he was alone in the house, August began to weep, tears of consternation and relief welled up and would not be contained, and he wept for a long while, tears coursing down his face as he sat on the edge of the bed, a quilt pulled around his body, for he was suddenly cold. It was not that the room was cold, for he had a small fire still burning, one Felix had made, but he was cold inside himself. Even his blood was cold, he imagined, and his bones. He couldn't understand himself; that was at the heart of his confusion.

In the afternoon, when he was sitting in his chair near the table, he looked out the door and saw Felix and Mr. Mooney Wright and one of Mr. Wright's sons, the older of his two natural sons, standing near the fence, looking at the place the cattle had got out. They came inside, peering before them cautiously. Mr. Wright sat down in

195

Sarah's chair. Felix brought in a log and set it on end, and he sat on that. The boy crouched by the fireplace. They had said hello and how are you, but August said nothing. He noticed none of them offered to shake his hand.

He watched them, much as a man who has been awakened from a drugged sleep. Fascinated, he noticed the spittle at the corner of Mr. Wright's mouth; he watched it foam and pulsate, as if breathing. The man was fifty-five, more or less, was stooped-shouldered, a healthy, thin, willow of a tough man, fibrous, handsome, with a strong face as yet without a line in it from age or wear.

"Been thinking about you, August," Mr. Wright said, and smiled briefly. "Wondering how you've been getting on."

"Yes," August said. "Well, I've been surprising myself in most every way."

"I hear you've taken several losses," Mr. Wright said. "First one and then another person has mentioned them."

"I'm left in dire shape, if the truth is known," August said.

"We're not here to blame you," Mr. Wright said calmly. "A calamity can come on any man. What we need to do at a time of need is gather around and help one another. That's what a community is."

"Yes, sir," August said.

"Olaf Singleterry came to see me this morning, determined to find this girl he owns. I told him years ago he ought to get rid of his slaves and tend to his own needs, and he said this morning he now saw that to be the truth, but that like most truths it had arrived too late to be of much use to him."

His speech had a touch of a soft, Southern accent to it, August noticed, but it was not a planter's accent. There was no apparent effort to persuade or to dominate anyone in his voice, yet power was there, and most of all, confidence.

"Olaf asked me about the girl, and I said, 'Olaf, she is not in this community anywhere, not in any house, barn, crib, shed, cave, not anywhere hereabouts, the best I know.' Olaf said he knew who must have her, and I said, 'Well, go see him and ask him for her, take her back home, do what you have to do to reclaim what's yours within the law.' And he said he would come by to get her, but I suppose he hasn't come yet, has he?" His gaze turned to August, the question poised before him.

"I've not seen him yet," August said.

"And she's not here?"

"No," August said.

"Well, there, you see, just as I told him," Mr. Wright said, relieved. "And you don't know where she is, do you, August?"

"I don't, no."

"There, you see," he said to his son and to Felix. "And you've not seen her anywhere along the way?"

"Oh, yes, I saw her."

Mr. Wright was caught awkwardly by the admission. He considered it speculatively, thoughtfully. "You saw her but you didn't help her—it's against the law to help her."

"I helped her," August said.

The three visitors considered that, the German moaning worriedly as he rocked back and forth on the log, Mr. Wright moodily pondering the seriousness of the matter, the boy nodding while calmly observing. "Oh my, my," the German said wearily.

Perhaps I should not have told them, August thought. But if I cannot trust these two men, what sort of loneliness will that leave me? They are my friends, such as I have, as are the wife of Felix and the daughter of Mr. Wright.

He watched the fire burn, the whiffs of smoke drift up from it, the solemn boy crouching beside it.

"There must be a hundred rumors about that girl, you know it?" Mr. Wright said, brightening. "I've not known a single other thing to gain so much notoriety so quickly. What day was it you went to market this year, anyway?"

"Seems like it was only this time last week," August replied.

"Last Monday morning," Felix said.

"And who helped you?"

"Felix helped me far as the Buffer field, where I hired two little worthless boys name of Howard and Loss who had brought a wagon up from Morganton for a man from Hawk."

"Drove mostly pigs?"

"Steers and pigs. I been thinking this afternoon I wish I had that big steer back. I would try to make a plow steer out of him. I tell you, Mr. Wright, I'll need a horse or steer or ox to work with around this place."

"Did you take anything else to sell?"

"Took eleven pounds of ginseng roots. Got fifty cents a pound for it. It was selling high."

"So was pigs high," Felix said.

"Yes, I did well this year," August admitted.

"Then you came back up the mountain, is that it?" Mr. Wright asked.

"That was Thursday, I guess it was. I was on the road by dawn and got to the ridgecrest by late afternoon. I went down to a creek to wash and saw this girl hiding in the rocks." He felt a knot in his throat, simply from remembering seeing her that first time. "Then I went to the Inn and paid off my mortgage."

"You did pay it?" Mr. Wright said.

"Yes, I have the deed all clear."

"Well, I'm glad of that. Somebody told me you probably hadn't done that, and I was worried to death about it. And Ama was," he said, mentioning his daughter's name with affection.

"No, I have it signed."

"Well, she'll certainly be relieved to hear that, as I am. You've done a world of good work here, August. You're a staunch man in this place, and we don't want to see you lose out here."

"Then I bought sugar and flour and powder."

"Yes. Now then, to get on with it, what else did you do?"

"Bought salt."

"Yes, but to get on with it, you saw the girl once more?"

"It was the next morning," August said, "near the ridgecrest gap. I went back to see her again. She had preyed on my mind so much, I wanted to get shut of her."

"Get shut of her by going back to see her?" Felix said.

"He went to tell her good-by," Mr. Wright said.

"And to feed her," August said.

"It's against the law to feed her—"

"As I would any beast or person in this world who's hungry," August said. "I will go a mile each way to feed an animal in a trap, if it's wounded and I can't get him out, won't I, Felix? I fed a coon down by the webbing of the creeks for three days, didn't I, Felix?"

"Four days, even though it was bound to die—"

"And what did you feed her?" Mr. Wright said.

"Fed her scraps."

"No, what did you feed the girl?"

"I never saw her. On this certain morning I never saw her."

"So then you came on toward home, is that it?" Mr. Wright said.

"Yes."

"There you come. I can see you myself. Your cart, your bags of supplies. Now there are those who say you had bought breeding stock at the market, but Felix says that's not so, that you never bought anything at all."

"I bought a milch cow, full-blooded Jersey. And a red boar, full-blooded."

"Well, where are they then?" Felix said.

"And three geese. I had all them with me that first day, but I didn't have the girl with me."

"Well, I—I'm—when did you come upon her?" Mr. Wright said.

"She arrived in the night," August said.

"Why not shoo her away? She's not fierce, I take it. It's against the law to harbor a runaway."

"I never thought to do it," August said.

"You never transported her, did you?" Mr. Wright

said. "There are those who tell us you had her in your cart all one day, and I have said to them, 'Well, he's not a fool; do you think he is a criminal and a fool?'"

"Well, she was in my cart all one day," August said. A long pause. The German cast a frightened look toward Mr. Wright, but the old man showed no sign of emotion at all, not even of surprise. His face was as stone. The boy's face was like his father's, revealing nothing.

"Maybe it's all true, even about the cow being killed and the boar being washed away," Mr. Wright said quietly to Felix. "I thought the girl must have come upon him here at his house, might have seen a window light. I never thought he would transport her."

"Did you bring her here, to Sarah's house?" Felix asked firmly.

"What do you mean, Sarah's house?" August said, flaring up angrily.

"You brought her here?" Felix asked.

"I brought her here, Felix," August said, "but not to Sarah's house."

"Listen at that, would you?" Felix said to Mr. Wright.

Mr. Wright nodded. "This morning two women came to my daughter and said, 'Ama, it's awful what August has done to you,' and I said, 'No, now, Ama, he never did a thing. You know August as well as I do.'"

August was affected by that comment, more even than by the others. "I never meant to hurt her," he said, "I never meant to hurt her."

"No? Well, what did you think would be said, with you harboring a nigger girl?"

"Mr. Wright, I swear I never meant it that way. I

never loved—I—don't suppose—I love anybody more than your daughter—"

"Well, do you love this nigger, is that it?"

"No. It's not that. She's not involved—"

"You tell Ama she's not involved, will you, when the women come to sympathize with her. Tell her about you and the nigger and break her heart," he said. For a while he considered that, his worry about his daughter. Abruptly he said, "I suppose you think I'm not involved either, but I am involved, because people come through my gate and say that the laws have been broken, the church has been insulted, the home has been desecrated, womankind has been ravaged, the dead have been denied, property has been stolen, a girl has been endangered, a boy has been slaughtered, all because of a man living here among us." Stern of voice like God Almighty's prophet, fierce anger in his eyes, his gaze focused on August unflinchingly.

And it was frightening, it tore into August's soul, the criticisms he had made. "It came over me, Mr. Wright, that's all I know to say," he said. "I did a hundred strange things and nothing customary. Will you explain it to me?"

"I can't explain anything like that—"

"I'm asking you to tell me. I've sat here all afternoon wondering to myself, asking where is my horse, what happened to my fence. I never killed a cow before yesterday in my life."

"I wouldn't think so," Mr. Wright said. "Not many of us have."

"I left my mare down by the creeks, tied to a tree branch for the whole of one night."

Mr. Wright leaned across the table toward him. "You wouldn't do that, surely."

"I've had that mare more than eight years. If there is any creature I love, it's that horse."

"Why, it's incredible that you would leave her—"

"I never questioned it at the time. My salt, my bag of salt fell out on the Buffer field, but I never even went back to get up what I could of it, and here I am without salt."

"Well, I declare," Mr. Wright said, astonished.

"I left three geese tied to a rope in the woods."

"My Lord," Mr. Wright said.

"I wonder as much as you what came over me. But I never questioned any of it during that day, Mr. Wright. It never dawned on me to wonder about anything. All of them seemed natural for me to do, yet everything I did was unusual for me. I've asked myself a thousand times today, I have sat here and said to myself, 'August, did you do that, did you do that?'"

"I never would have believed it of you," Felix said.

"It was a fever had me, something like a fever. I had to get that girl through that net of dangers and to my own house here—"

"To ravish her, was it?" Felix said sternly.

"No."

"Did you ravish her?"

"No."

"In Sarah's bed?" the German asked.

"Why is it Sarah's bed?"

"She comforted you in that bed for six years, bore you a child in it," Felix said.

"I didn't touch the girl. My father never even touched a black in his—"

"You gave her all Sarah's things, for some reason."

"I gave her all Sarah's things, but not for any reason I know of."

Felix fell silent, frowning at August, a deep, pouting resentment troubling him.

"I wonder where she is now, you know it, not that I ever expect to see her again. I miss her."

"Sarah, you miss Sarah?" Felix asked.

"Oh, yes, I missed Sarah for a long while." He said nothing more. He watched the boy's somber face, his jaw chewing on something or other, perhaps a spice-bush stem, the fire beside him.

"It's so that sometimes a madness temporarily falls on a body," Mr. Wright said evenly, considerately.

"Fell on that Curtis daughter," Felix said.

"Thought she was a dog," Mr. Wright admitted. "Crawled around on all-fours on the ground, barked for her food, lapped up water with her tongue."

"Let a dog mount her," Felix said.

"No, no, no, I don't think so," Mr. Wright said. "Now that rumor was started by Ellie Marland, who always has been jealous of her—"

"A bird dog," Felix said.

"I don't think so, Felix."

"Been other signs and spells. Devils riding people up and down the roads—" Felix said.

"Now, now, Felix, we must retain our own even senses, or we can't help here at all."

"Senses? I've known August for eight years, since he arrived up here, and he has never one day done anything the least bit different from what he did the day before. Poor Sarah used to confess to me that he was so staunch in his ways that she wept— I'm telling him the truth, August—"

"She was the one who was boring to live with," August said.

"Sarah told me over and over—"

"It's not so," August said.

"Now, I'll have no more talk about her, that one," Mr. Wright said. "She's not involved in this." He waited until the quiet had settled in the room, then sat back in the chair, seeking a more comfortable position, moaning softly, fretfully annoyed.

He must worry about this whole community, August thought, the place he has made of stone and logs and families and stock and held together over the years. He is wondering about the reputation of the place and the value of his unsold land, I suspect. And about his daughter. I know he loves her more than anybody else in the world, because she depends on him more than does anybody else in the world; he is a man with hundreds of dependents, he needs dependents and honors them, protects them. What does he think of me, now that I have left the fold he guards. I wonder, should he close his eyes, if he could say the color of my hair, of my eyes, the shape, whether oval or round, long or broad, of my face. I am yet another person in a mass of people who must be kept in strict account always, lest the whole slip from him. I am a torn stitch that might unravel the cloth he has for thirty years been weaving.

The boy watches me, too, all too closely; it embarrasses me. His gaze is unrevealing when he watches his father, but there is worship in his eyes when he looks at me. Annoying. Will he and other young people now follow me on the road and say to one another, "There he goes, the one who brought that brown waif up the road, outwitted everyone."

The hot gaze of Felix also was on him. He felt that Felix was trying to penetrate into his mind, into the boiling mass of his brains to see if he was sane or insane, possessed or not. What would Felix hope to find? Jealousy was his chief self-torture, so he would hope for some malady or other. He is jealous even now, even of my notoriety and pain, August thought. He has always been jealous of me. He is a false friend, I know, but a companion. If a man cannot have friends, then let him, please God, have companions.

"I worry about myself," August said suddenly. "I can see into others better than I can see into myself."

Mr. Wright grunted, an absent-minded acknowledgment. "Now," he said gently, "what say we try to prepare a defense?"

Is there to be a trial? August thought, not daring to ask Mr. Wright. No, surely there would not be a trial way up here, he decided. Then is there to be a punishment meted out to me—a beating, he wondered. No, not up here. Not to a white man, a neighbor, certainly.

"We must try to pull the elements together," Mr. Wright said. "Tell me, how did your cart come to be at Hobbs?"

"I don't know," August said. "Somebody must have stolen it and driven it down there."

"Were you not taking the girl home to Olaf, who lives nearby?" Mr. Wright said.

"No, no," August said. "I would never do that."

"Now, take your time deciding on where the truth lies," Mr. Wright said. He sniffed and wiped his mouth with his hand. "Truth has no skin, no appearance, it doesn't cling to the surface, not that I ever saw." He coughed, a dry, raspy sound. "Think before you reply."

August said nothing; he had no idea what Mr. Wright expected of him, and he had not much confidence in his own thoughts just now anyway.

"You didn't have the girl with you on the road; we can insist on that, for Olaf himself told me he looked into your cart. Also two hunters told me they were watching at the Buffer's field, as were many others, so obviously you never had her with you there. As for the loss of your new cow, I expect many a person would have stolen a Jersey cow and, once word went out that she was stolen, the thief might have had to abandon her to save himself from being found out. As for the boar, somebody this morning said you were caught in the river's current yourself—"

"He was lame," Felix said. "Somebody said the boar was lame."

"The boar was lame, very well," Mr. Wright said. "You didn't want him. Then you were coming along the road to this community, where you are a leader, a church leader, where you are known by everybody to be a substantial landowner, a builder, a citizen who has never broken a law. I can imagine you were coming home when this runaway girl came busting out of the bushes, and you did what any decent body would do, you agreed to take her to her home. She consented—tearfully, I imagine—and you came on down that little

207

trail to the three-creek fords, the girl in tow—"

"The geese," Felix said.

"Forget the geese for now," Mr. Wright said, "and you lost your cart wheel in the second, third creek, and since you had all your supplies in the cart, you said to the girl, 'I'll leave the cart here, leave the horse tied, and you and me will carry such flour and sugar as we can—' "

"Why did he leave the horse?" Felix said.

"I don't know why he left the horse," Mr. Wright said irritably.

"Somebody's going to ask, Olaf or—"

"There are bound to be loose ends to any honest account," Mr. Wright said.

"The geese and the horse—" Felix began.

"Forget the geese," Mr. Wright said, "he never had any geese, they flew away up on the ridge some'ers, I saw them myself, flying away, everybody saw the geese flying away. Nobody will burn this man's house and sheds down because of three geese."

Silence fell, a hush came over them all, the warning itself had flashed fire in the room, leaving its own vibrations and rumblings.

"Burn my house?" August said.

"Not if we go along together as a community, explain what happened," Mr. Wright said calmly. "Burning's what they warn me will happen, that's all. Never mind about that just now—"

"Burn my house?"

"Unless the horse is explained," Felix said, "they might decide—"

"Yes, yes. Well, I don't know about the horse. I suppose the horse was stolen when August was called into the woods by the girl. He came out to take her to Olaf and saw that the horse was stolen, and he said to her to help him carry his powder and sugar home, his coffee, whatever it was—"

"Flour," Felix suggested.

"And while they were on that mission, then the cart was stolen."

"I understand," Felix said. "That explains most everything. Except—"

"Yes, I know, but let the geese be. Let a few loose ends hang."

August shook his head anxiously. "It's confusing to hear you talk this way," he said. "I know you have to explain—"

"It's all so involved, so many people involved," Mr. Wright said, "the anger's so high—and the truth is hid most often, as something dropped off a vessel in a storm might never be found, then again it might someday float to shore. No time to wait for it all."

"The truth is not what you say," August said.

"No, and it's not what you say, either," Mr. Wright said, "for your truth is merely one incident after another, not the truth at all, for truth is not an incident. Now you leave it to me, you hear?"

"I—all right." August sat back wearily in his chair.

"The truth is never easy to locate in an emergency," Mr. Wright said. "You were trying to help somebody, and at personal expense, so why should you be punished for that? Is that the truth of it?"

"That's true," Felix said.

"All of us want to do all we can for you," Mr. Wright said.

"He will let you help him," Felix said. "It won't hurt him or the girl to do that. I tell you, if they burn him out, it'll leave Mina and me alone up here."

"Yes. Well," Mr. Wright said wearily. He sat with lowered head and pursed lips, staring at the hearth, sniffing now and then.

August felt a stirring of affection for him. There was inside that craggy body a mind and heart of considerable power, and the man tried to be fair in all he did. "Can it be forgot?" he asked suddenly, anxious to know, not that he was certain he wanted it to be forgot but that he wanted to know if he had the choice.

A pause, Felix watching the old man, staring at him, not replying, for he had no clue what would be expected of him to say; the boy by the fireplace watching his father's face; the old man rousing himself finally. "Oh, yes," he said gently.

A long quiet then. It was decided, done. The boy shifted his leg, which must have got strained. Mr. Wright scratched his neck and shoulder unconcernedly. "What a human being will get himself into sometimes," he murmured. He belched. "My stomach is the thermometer of my body," he said quietly. "Got so I have to have two Dr. Dyott's pills every night, this community is becoming so large and strained." He spit into the fireplace. "I will help you for Ama's sake, and my own," he said gently. "After all, it could have happened to most any one of us."

The two hunters arrived just before twilight began, and took places near the crib, where they crouched, their backs against the crib wall. They told Felix they didn't care to come in. They would not be interested in explanations or confessions or denials; it was the work, after the decisions were made, that would interest them.

Mr. Wright and August still sat near the table, watching the fire, August's mind revolving fitfully, now and then drawing away from any denial at all, grasping at affirmation. You don't want to lose the credit for what you did, August, he told himself. Yet, having the credit wasn't it, wasn't at the heart of it. The girl had a right to an affirmation, to a friend. Even here, even here. Yet the girl was gone.

The boy, crouched at the fireplace wall, was intently watching August's face. His gaze would go now and then to his father's face, then he would watch August for a long while. He seemed to be evaluating the worth of both men.

Felix was talking. "The Bible tells us about evil spirits. I know myself that Mina one day she was pretty and youthful, next day she was wan and her flesh began to waxen. It was a curse on her, I imagine. I've not felt the same toward her since. Now we have as strange a case in its way, except it's a man. Thank God he's in our care, or what might he do next? Anybody who will tie three geese to a rope—"

"Forget the geese, Felix," Mr. Wright said sleepily. "It never happened."

"And lose his supplies for the year," Felix said, "with

no salt or sugar in his house. He'll need a plow-brute of some sort, Mr. Wright."

"I'll loan him a horse," Mr. Wright said.

"And salt, so he can cure meat," Felix said.

"Yes. All right. Ama can help him with such chores this year."

"He will need a cook pot," Felix said.

"Ama will give him one," Mr. Wright said.

"Tell Ama I never meant to hurt her, not in this world," August said suddenly.

"No, now," Mr. Wright said gently. "You let me explain it to everyone, you hear?" Gently, as to a frightened man, he spoke. "Ama talks about you all the time, August, most every day finds some way to mention your name, and she's a fine judge of character, I believe."

Olaf arrived before dark, though the sky was reddening by then. Three men were with him, but he was the only one who came inside the house. He looked about critically, standing near the doorway until his eyes had adjusted to the darkness of the room. He noticed Felix first, then Mr. Wright. He saw the boy. Then he saw August, and a groan came out of him, an angry gasp. "You have her?" he said.

All of them sat there waiting, August holding his breath, sitting with his hands clenched, feeling small and disabled and unable in the shadow of the power all around him, seeing himself in the shadow of old meetings of planters and farmers, of Harristown and Hobbs, of free and slave, fire and blood.

"No, we've not found her," Mr. Wright said finally, his voice taking on a mournful, regretful tone. "She was here for a few minutes last night, and then she ran off into those bushes toward my house."

"She's not here?" Olaf whispered incredulously. "My God, is she not here?"

"She was here for a few minutes last night," Mr. Wright said, "helped this poor man carry some goods up from his cart, then she ran off into the bushes toward my house."

"Ahhhhhh," Olaf said, and shook his head anxiously. "You don't have her, you say?" he said to August.

"No, Olaf, he don't have her," Mr. Wright answered.

Olaf came closer. August now could see the perspiration gathered in drops on his face, could smell the brandy and tobacco on him.

"I won't accept it," Olaf said. "I will accept her, that's all. No arguments, no explanations, and I'll agree to ask for none later, but the girl I'll have."

"She's not here, Olaf," Mr. Wright said calmly. "As I told you, the girl is not here."

"You said you would get her for me."

"She is not here to be got," Mr. Wright said.

Olaf came still closer to where August was, looked down directly into his eyes. "Where is she?"

"Now, there's no need to create a scene," Mr. Wright said evenly, patiently. "We have talked with this poor man for a long while, and I assure you she is not here, she was not here except for a minute or two last night, and he has not—as you know yourself, for you told me you had examined his cart—"

This poor man, August thought. Mr. What's-his name.

"Please, will you?" Olaf said, looking at August, a pain of deep suffering on him, shuddering through him, anguish bending his shoulders. "Please. Where is she?"

"He can't tell you that, Olaf," Mr. Wright said gently.

"Tell me, did you see her? Where did you see her?"

"At the creek I first saw her," August said calmly, "three evenings ago, near the gap; when I went down to bathe myself, I saw her standing back in the rocks and felt sorry for her then, and for myself . . ." He told it all, every detail of it, he told even that he had given her clothes to wear, while Olaf listened, while all of them listened, amazed.

"It's all the same piece of cloth," August later told Felix and the boy. The other men were outdoors now, standing in the soggy yard, discussing what ought to be done here. It was twilight. "I still can't deny her, or myself," August said. "I don't want to be only what I was, Felix. I have reached the autumn of my life and need to breathe free."

Outside Mr. Wright was saying, "It all started when his wife died, and his mind, as you see, was warped by it. Every decision he has made for three days further endangers him. You can't trust him to tell the truth. He's not accountable, Olaf."

"I'm the one who got free," August said to Felix and the boy.

Outdoors Mr. Wright was saying, "Well, burn him out, if that will please you. It seems not to matter to him, so why ought it to matter to me? I wash my hands of him."

"Where's my girl is what I want to know," Olaf said.

"He's bound to have set her on a trail out of here," somebody said.

"There's only one," somebody said.

"I thought he had her yet," Olaf said.

"Ahhhh, he's got a prophet's outlook on him and

cares not one whit for property," Mr. Wright said
fiercely.

August heard their footsteps on the muddy ground,
the squishing of the feet of the men. Somebody said, "I
expect the rain has washed off ever trace, don't you?"

"I have no more use for him, as you can imagine," Mr.
Wright was saying. "What can anybody do for such a
man in a community?"

Felix put a log on the cabin fire, then sat back wearily
in the chair. "I don't know what I'll tell Mina about it,
or what she'll believe."

"No, it's not all of it explainable," August said gently.

"I'll stay with you as long as I think I can, August,"
Felix said, "though you are a stranger to me. I wonder
where my old friend is, the one I knew for eight years,
who worked beside me, was thoughtful of every decision. Why, that daughter of his has a dowry, I suspect,
more than enough—your sister I mean," Felix said to
the boy.

The boy nodded without speaking.

"You suppose Mr. Wright is right, that Sarah's death
was the start of it?" Felix said. When August didn't
reply, he said, "What did she say to you, August, that
last day, before she fell?"

"The day she killed herself?" August said to him.

"Killed herself?" Felix said, stunned. "Why, she
never would have done that."

"She came into this room where I was eating bread
and told me she was going to bear a child in the summer, and I began to complain about it, about not being
certain the baby would live, about my worry lest we go
through the horrors of a baby illness again, about my

not knowing whether the child would be mine or whether it was yours."

"What say?" Felix said, whispering. "What say?"

"We talked about it, shouting and shuddering one to another, until she left through that door, and the best I could tell she was crying."

"Awful," Felix said, choking.

"Yes, it was, and I have regretted it every day since. I have wished to God I had said instead, 'Sarah, this is not a matter for us to argue about, as we do most else day by day; this is a matter of life and goes beyond that.' But once she had killed herself—"

"Awful, August, to say to me—to say she killed herself."

"Well, Lord knows, Felix, she was like a mountain goat for footholds. She never slipped one time in seven years of farming on this rocky place, and what do you think she went way up there for anyway? There's no work to do up there, and she never was one to care about prospects."

"To say I had—as if I had anything to do with—"

"Oh, yes, we both thrashed about in our shallow streambeds and killed her, that's the truth of it."

"Awful," Felix said. "I scarcely know you, August," he said, moving away from him. He stopped at the door, hesitated on the edge of speech, but said nothing else and stumbled on down the hill, following Mr. Wright and Olaf Singleterry, who were walking down toward the village road, shouting at one another, three men with them, arguing among themselves about what was proper for them to do.

The two hunters, laughing at some thought they

must have shared, walked on up through August's field, toward the high road the girl had used.

The darkness began to gather before August moved. "I never did do much in my life, before here lately," he said gently. "I suppose I was never asked by anybody."

The Wright boy still crouched by the fireplace, watching him. "There's likely to be more of them run off, now she's got away," he said softly. "Don't you think so?"

"I don't know," August said. "Do you think so?"

"I expect," the boy said. He was only about fourteen, about her age, Annalees' age. "It's like a knife," he said, "that trail through the wilderness. It's the best way for them to use."

"I don't know," August said. "I've never thought much about it."

The boy stood and slowly came closer. "They'll need food and direction."

"I suppose so. But I've done what I had to do, nothing more and nothing less," August said. "Somebody else will need to do for them."

"Yes," the boy said softly. He stood for a long while staring into August's eyes, before he reached forward and touched with his bare hand the bare flesh of August's face.

When it was dark, this being the third day, August took Sarah's herbs out of doors and scattered them on her grave. He stood in the field for a while, stood alone waiting for the moon to clear itself of clouds so he could see what would come of the night, if any of the men were to return or not, and so he could say good night to them all, the graves and to her.

"It's a good night for you to travel, Anna," he said to the wind. "Move on, move on, little girl, to the north country."

He sat down on a rock slab he had but this past spring, with his mare's lungings, broke free from the hill, and which he had been meaning ever since to pull on down into the yard. "I tell you, Sarah, it has been an unaccountable day for arguments," he said. "I have felt more strangeness today than on a sad Christmas."

He sat there considering that, smiling whimsically, bemused by the notion, and for a while he said nothing more; then he straightened. "But I tell you," he said to the graves and the wind, "I've never been so proud."

71 72 73 10 9 8 7 6 5 4 3 2 1